KING'S PROMISED PRINCESS

LYNNE GRAHAM

Recycling programs for this product may not exist in your area.

ISBN-13: 978-1-335-61401-8

King's Promised Princess

For questions and comments about the quality of this book, please contact us at CustomerService@Harlequin.com.

Harlequin Enterprises ULC
22 Adelaide St. West, 41st Floor
Toronto, Ontario M5H 4E3, Canada
www.Harlequin.com

HarperCollins Publishers
Macken House, 39/40 Mayor Street Upper,
Dublin 1, D01 C9W8, Ireland
www.HarperCollins.com

Printed in Lithuania

1 2 3 4 5 6 7 8 9 10 LIT 28 27 26 25

"You're so sure you know best, so certain of yourself…it's very annoying."

"I'm not about to apologize." Perfect white teeth flashed in a half smile. For a split second, Orazio looked so stunningly handsome that Zia couldn't take her eyes off him. Those amazing green eyes, that astonishing bone structure, the fine dark brows and lush black curling lashes. Anyone else with that shade of blond hair would have inherited blond or sandy brows and lashes, but Orazio had naturally got black to accentuate his already very striking eyes.

"You can relax, Orazio. I don't want to marry you either," Zia told him boldly, amused by the way he froze in surprise at her frankness. "I don't want to be a queen any more than I really want to be a princess, but becoming a princess was my way out of a difficult situation."

"You are a minx, Your Highness. A woman has never told me before that she doesn't want to marry me."

Lynne Graham was born in Northern Ireland and has been a keen romance reader since her teens. She is very happily married to an understanding husband who has learned to cook since she started to write! Her five children keep her on her toes. She has a very large dog who knocks everything over, a very small terrier who barks a lot and two cats. When time allows, Lynne is a keen gardener.

Books by Lynne Graham

Harlequin Presents

Two Secrets to Shock the Italian
His Royal Bride Replacement
Shock Greek Heir

Cinderella Sisters for Billionaires

The Maid Married to the Billionaire
The Maid's Pregnancy Bombshell

The Diamond Club

Baby Worth Billions

The Diamandis Heirs

Greek's Shotgun Wedding
Greek's One-Night Babies

Billion-Dollar Bride Swap

Unveiling the Wrong Bride
Her Two Greek Secrets

Visit the Author Profile page
at Harlequin.com for more titles.

KING'S PROMISED PRINCESS

CHAPTER ONE

'WHAT DO *YOU* think would tempt the Princess into returning here, Your Majesty?' the government special advisor, Massimo Caccia, pressed in frustration. 'We're not having any luck with her. The people want her back here because of her saintly mother and her reputation... as if she'd be some sort of good-luck symbol. Mandovia really *needs* her to be part of this deal.'

'I don't know her,' Orazio, generally known as Raz to his friends, countered levelly, unable to avoid the reality that he thoroughly disliked the older man for his specious manners. Usually, he was very much the smoothie politician but the aggressive soldier he had been showed through too often.

'You're the only one of this generation who has even met her, Your Majesty,' Massimo pointed out.

'I was ten years old and she was a toddler of three,' Orazio reminded him. 'I can only tell you that she was a little girl who liked to climb trees—'

'But your father and hers arranged a betrothal between you.'

Raz breathed in so deep and long to suppress his exasperation that his executive assistant, Fiero, planted a deft hand on his arm as though to restrain his sovereign. 'Agreed, but I doubt that even back then either my father or the dictator ever thought their little gentlemen's agreement would become anything more than an expression of goodwill between neighbouring countries.'

'I disagree,' Massimo argued vehemently. 'The dictator knew his days were numbered and he had no son. He hoped that announcing that betrothal would satisfy the revolutionaries that change was truly on the horizon.'

'You could be right,' Fiero slotted in lightly.

'I'm rarely wrong.' Massimo smirked and it took years of court training for Raz to resist the urge to roll his eyes. 'And resurrecting that betrothal now would delight many people.'

It would not delight Orazio but he did not waste his time saying so. 'You're chasing a fairy tale, Massimo. You already know everything there is to know about Princess Annunziata. She's in London and apparently content to work there as a chambermaid. The government offered her an all-expenses-paid trip to Mandovia and she ignored the invitation. When they tried to visit her home, the door was slammed in their faces. Upper Mandovians killed her father and Lower Mandovians killed her mother. Maybe she simply wants to *forget* her heritage—'

'Her mother's death was a horrible accident at the border and everyone accepts that!' Massimo protested in an angry, defensive tone that reminded everybody present that he had been a military commander during that troubled period. 'It offends Upper Mandovians that their Princess should be living in such reduced circumstances and the Princess owes a duty of responsibility towards her people at a time when they *need* that reassurance.'

Orazio released his breath in a slow, measured hiss. 'Annunziata left this country at the age of three. She wasn't raised with such concepts. Who knows what horrors she saw in the street-fighting the night that her mother's companion fled with her?'

Massimo, a thickset rather portly male, rose to his feet heavily. 'If she were here and willing, *would* you marry her, Your Majesty?' he demanded with startling abruptness.

The prime minister, a small, slight, older male very much less vigorous in personality than his advisor, also stood up and cleared his throat in the smouldering silence. 'I don't think it's fair to ask our King to answer such a question about a woman he's never met.'

'If both she and my people wanted it, I would do it,' Orazio ground out with the chilling hauteur of extreme reluctance. 'But, short of a miracle, I don't believe that situation will ever arise.'

'I apologise,' the prime minister murmured uncomfortably as his advisor stomped out of the room, ignoring all court protocol. 'Massimo gets on his favourite hobby horse and forgets who you are. He's obsessed with getting the Princess back on her home soil and that betrothal nonsense. But he does mean well. He's devoted to our country and he's desperate for the reunification to continue smoothly.'

'As are we all,' Orazio conceded easily, thinking that it had still taken almost twenty years for the rudimentary, inexperienced revolutionary government in Upper Mandovia to agree to the reintegration of the two parts of Mandovia that should never have been separated in the first place. The upper part was landlocked, staunchly traditional and very poor, the lower rich and prosperous. The dictator, Annunziata's late and unlamented father, Octavio Giordano, had denied his people the education, medical care and opportunities freely available in the kingdom next door. Eventually the people themselves had risen up to overthrow Octavio and reclaim democracy.

'I don't like Massimo,' Raz breathed as he and Fiero trudged back across the castle to the monarch's private accommodation. 'He's sly and scheming.'

'Nobody likes him,' Fiero chuckled. 'He can be very rude. I don't know how you kept your temper, Raz.'

'The prime minister was as red in the face as a tomato,' Raz sighed. 'I felt sorry for him. He has to cope with Massimo every day. I see him only once a month or so. I'm fortunate.'

'Sometimes, I don't know why you took on this gig,' his childhood friend and executive assistant admitted.

'Or why you accompanied me and left the business world behind where you were flourishing? For the same reasons as my own,' Raz replied with confidence. 'First and foremost, this is *our* country and we want to do the best we can for it and steer it in the right direction.'

'But you never wanted to be King—'

'I didn't expect to have people begging me to come back and step into my father's shoes. Not only did I think the monarchy would eventually be abolished, but I also didn't expect my father to die in his fifties,' Orazio acknowledged, a bleak look in the emerald-green eyes, so bright against his bronzed skin and the caramel-blond contrast of his hair. 'I was content in my life but here I'm not just making money, I can really make a difference and push reforms through by engaging the right people in the process.'

'Your mother's still in shock that you accepted the throne.'

'She has her take on Mandovia and I have mine.' His mother, Luisa, had separated from his father years before their split became public. She had refused to live with a cheating husband and, once the word was out, she had returned to her native Venezuela and the family diamond mines, happily rediscovering the wealthy socialite lifestyle she had lost when she'd married. Bitter years spent in an unhappy marriage had left her with a strong aversion to anything related to Mandovia.

Orazio, conversely, had been forced to live between two worlds and several countries from the day of his parents' official separation. He had been schooled in business by his billionaire grandfather for one half of the year and schooled in the monarchy for the other half. If anything, his father's corruption had given Raz a distaste for hereditary rulership. The former King Luciano had been much more interested in feathering his own nest than in instigating a benevolent reign aimed at stabilising Mandovia under one unifying figurehead.

Even so, his parents' talent for schmoozing the rich into investing in Lower Mandovia had been unparalleled. As a result Lower Mandovia was as rich as Upper Mandovia was poor and those glaring inequalities were unacceptable in the twenty-first century. That challenge was precisely why Orazio had finally agreed to accept the throne, although it had not occurred to him then that one day a government official would dare to demand that he marry a total stranger.

'What do you remember about Annunziata?' Fiero asked him curiously.

'She was a very cute toddler when she wasn't kicking or scratching me,' Orazio recalled with a sudden laugh. 'She was in a tree and her nursemaid couldn't get her down. At the maid's request, I lifted her down and, even though she was really tiny, she fought me like a tigress, ripping her fancy dress and shouting at the top of her voice. She reminded me more of a wild animal than a princess...'

'Suffice it to say that she could never be your dream match,' Fiero quipped. 'You like sophisticated, tranquil women. In any case, she works as a chambermaid. She couldn't cut it here in this world and you've never lived anything other than a very privileged life. You'd be oil and water.'

'Don't be weird,' Orazio urged, disliking the tone of the conversation as he poured both of them a drink. He wondered if Fiero knew just how snobbish he sounded. Harvey, his father's much-prized English butler and the major domo of the current King's household, frowned at them both from the doorway. 'Go away,' Orazio told the older man quietly. 'You're still supposed to be on medical leave after your surgery. You shouldn't be coming downstairs to serve us drinks.'

'You are royal, Your Majesty,' Harvey reminded him stubbornly. 'You do *not* need to serve your own drinks.'

'Unlike my father, I'm a modern monarch. I don't expect to be waited on hand and foot like some feudal king.'

'Nonetheless and with respect,' Harvey responded heavily, 'you *are* the King and it is your place to be served by staff and *my* place and *my* honour to wait on you, Your Majesty.'

'And that's us told,' Orazio quipped as the door closed on Harvey's censorious exit. 'Poor Harvey, sentenced to wait on a king who still doesn't know his place.'

'He learnt his role under your father, and your father wouldn't have got off his feet to do anything for himself,' Fiero pointed out with amusement. 'Your problem is too much compassion and, according to Harvey, that's not your role.'

'But if it isn't, what is?' Orazio asked ruefully.

Zia hurtled through the door of the basement flat and bestowed a fleeting kiss on the top of the greying head of the older woman wrapped in a blanket in an armchair, knitting. 'Sorry I'm late. I had to do Sandrine's shopping for her supper party tonight.'

'I forgot about that. You should tell her how tired you are after your shift at the hotel,' Alina suggested, but she did so in a lacklustre undertone, already foreseeing how such a remark would be received by Sandrine.

As an excitable miniature dachshund danced round Zia's feet in welcome, flapping ears flying, pink tongue licking at her hand as she patted him, Zia laughed. Her former nursemaid and her pet were the two bright spots in her dreary day. After all, she didn't get to put her feet up when she got home after work. No, she simply worked for Sandrine instead—Sandrine, once her guardian, who now treated her like a servant.

As Alina had aged and become less capable, Zia had taken over the older woman's duties of cooking for Sandrine and cleaning her house upstairs. If she had refused, Sandrine would have thrown Alina out on the street. Alina didn't seem to appreciate how often Sandrine had made that threat or that the tough older woman meant what she said. And while Zia believed she could have coped, she didn't earn enough to take care of Alina as well or Sausage, the little dog who had become theirs.

Over the years, Alina had gradually become Zia's family and the closest thing she had ever had to a grandmother. In the space of months after the revolution that had killed her parents, Zia had gone from being a much-indulged only child to a battered little girl and a shadow of her former self. Sandrine Beccari might have willingly ferried the little Princess, who had been born in London, to the safety of the UK but she hadn't expected the tragedies that had followed and she certainly hadn't planned to be saddled for years with the responsibility of a young child.

Temperamentally unsuited to parenting, Sandrine had fiercely resented Zia's existence and the loss of her glamorous life in Mandovia at the late Princess Vittoria's side. She had taken her temper and disappointment out on Zia, and Alina, subjected to similar abuse as a lifelong servant in backward Upper Mandovia, had proved incapable of protecting her former charge. Life had only improved for the two of them when they had been forced to move into the small damp basement flat. It had been cheaply renovated for tenants, but the tenants had infuriated Sandrine with their complaints and had made too much noise. Getting rid of them, she had been relieved to turf Alina and Zia out of her much more comfortable house upstairs while continuing to expect Zia to act as free labour. And since they couldn't afford to pay Sandrine rent for the flat, how was she ever supposed to break free of the arrangement?

In reality, Zia did *have* an escape plan but it was taking time to accomplish her goals. Currently it entailed getting the education that Sandrine had denied her by insisting that she be homeschooled. Zia had pretty much educated herself because Alina, put in charge of that home-based programme, had left school at the age of fourteen to start work and had only ever learned the basics. Year after year, once Zia was officially out in the working world, she had studied for exams to acquire the qualifications she needed to get into college. It was a slow process, however, because she didn't have much free time to study.

At twenty-two years of age, she had only recently reached the stage where she could even apply for further education and she dreaded taking on the loans she would need to allow her to become a student. But it would be worth it, she kept on telling herself, because once she qualified as a primary school teacher she would be earning and then her real life could begin.

She barely recalled the life she had been born into, wincing at the truth that she was a princess only on paper, a title that meant nothing in terms of cold, hard cash or respect. Her mother was a perfumed memory of warmth but she still remembered her father shouting and slapping her away from him when she knocked over a cup and then her mother scooping her up and murmuring loving words in comfort. Zia had been careful to stay out of her father's way after that. The much feared and loathed dictator of Upper Mandovia had not been any kinder in his domestic life.

'We have a Mandovian guest at the hotel right now,' Zia informed Alina, knowing that that rare event would engage the older woman's interest.

'If she's staying at the Astor Place she must be a very rich woman. What's her name?' Alina asked, dark eyes sparkling with curiosity.

'Sofia Marone and she has a maid travelling with her. I heard them speaking Italian and referring to Lower Mandovia's capital city while I was changing the bathroom towels and the maid kept on calling her mistress "my lady", so she must be someone titled.'

Alina frowned and hummed, 'Marone… Marone. There was a count with that family name. I suspect that'll be the connection.'

The older woman embarked on an animated recitation of what she knew of the Marone family history and perked up considerably while deciding that the hotel guest was very probably the wealthy count's second wife. Zia made their evening meal in the tiny scullery and served it on trays before heading upstairs, laden with groceries and receipts, to embark on the supper-party preparations. The connecting door brought her straight into Sandrine's sleek contemporary kitchen, which as usual required cleaning before she could prepare the dish that had been requested.

The click of Sandrine's stiletto heels approaching stiffened Zia's spine to steel. 'What are you making?' she demanded imperiously.

'Chicken Alfredo.'

'And for dessert?'

'I'm not making one. You said it was a casual gathering to drink wine and play cards. I brought the snacks and the wine but I won't be able to stay and serve it. I have a class tonight.'

'That's not acceptable!' Sandrine hissed and Zia spun round.

'I'm afraid it has to be. I keep your house clean, do the washing, the shopping and I cook whenever you ask. Surely that's sufficient to cover us not paying rent,' she responded, quelling her instinctive fear of the older woman.

A tall, emaciated brunette in a skintight black dress, her red-lipsticked mouth pursed, Sandrine glowered down at her. 'I decide what's sufficient, *not* you. Have you any idea how much rent you should be paying me?'

'It's a damp one-bedroom flat with heating that doesn't work, not a palace,' Zia dared, tilting her chin, which took courage because she was five feet one inch tall and, in her heels, Sandrine was almost a foot taller than her.

'How *dare* you speak to me like that?' Sandrine launched, half an octave higher.

'I do almost everything you ask me to do,' Zia responded quietly. 'I do work for a living as well.'

'Poor little princess,' the brunette sneered. 'And more fool me that I've kept you all these years! I should've handed you over to social services and thrown that old crippled crone out years ago! Instead, out of the goodness of my heart, I looked after you both at my own expense.'

'I'll leave everything prepared for you,' Zia promised soothingly. 'And clean up tomorrow.'

'I'm thinking of advertising for live-in help to take your place.' Sandrine dropped the news on her with a razor-edged smile. 'Someone properly trained as a housekeeper.'

Zia nodded in silence, not trusting herself to speak. It was pointless engaging with Sandrine when she was in a temper or making threats. The older woman had little self-control and Zia was careful not to invite assault. She had suffered quite enough violence from Sandrine while she was growing up and she refused to stand for it as an adult.

'Nothing to say to that?' Sandrine prompted provocatively as she strolled back to the door.

'Of course not, you must do as you wish,' Zia breathed before turning back to the sink to finish her task.

The dish prepared, she set out plates and cutlery and a note with cooking instructions on reheating. Returning to the basement, she grabbed her file and headed out to her class on early child development. Later that evening she fell into her bed across the small, cramped room from Alina, exhausted, and contemplated her early start the next day with a stoic grimace.

Late morning in the hotel, she was waiting to clean the last luxury suite on her schedule when one of the doors in the hallway flew open and the young woman she had identified as a maid gesticulated fiercely at her. 'Come here!' she shouted.

Abandoning her trolley, Zia approached. 'What's happened?' she asked anxiously.

'My employer has misplaced a valuable diamond brooch!' she exclaimed. 'Help us look for it…come on, what are you waiting for?'

Zia really didn't want to get involved but it was management policy to always try to please guests and, mastering her reluctance, she stepped into the suite where the guest, surrounded by designer shopping bags, was frantically tipping out drawers in a dresser to search for her missing jewellery.

Zia got down on her hands and knees to check under the furniture, while wondering where the maid had gone. 'Did you see my brooch when you were in here earlier making the bed?' the guest demanded.

'No, there were items sitting on the dressing table but I didn't go over to them or touch anything. I cleaned, changed the bed and put fresh towels in the en suite,' she recounted.

The young maid stalked in. 'Have her trolley searched! She must've been in here while we were out,' she condemned.

And then there was a whole fracas with Zia steadily proclaiming her blamelessness, various other guests appearing to ask what was going on and then finally the manager arrived looking world-weary and put upon.

'My brooch has gone. The girl's trolley should be searched,' the guest insisted, treating Zia to a suspicious appraisal.

The manager told her to bring her trolley in and Zia retrieved it with resentment mounting high inside her small frame. On request, she unloaded the trolley, stacking soiled towels into an untidy heap, and when she reached the final one, as she shook it out, something bright and glittering fell out and clinked on the polished floor. It was a big brooch. Astonished, Zia froze while the manager stooped to pick it up and show it to the guest, who swiftly identified it and pinned it to her jacket.

As accusing eyes settled on Zia, she reddened. 'I've never seen it before. I didn't touch it or take it,' she said through taut lips, her face as rigid as the rest of her.

'We'll discuss this downstairs in my office,' the manager announced.

'I want the police called. I want the thief to be arrested and punished,' the guest declared fiercely. 'What sort of hotel are you running that a guest's jewellery can be stolen by one of your staff?'

'I didn't steal it,' Zia murmured again but everyone simply ignored her.

She sat in the waiting area outside the manager's officer while the angry guest chattered in her own language as she rang the Mandovian Embassy for assistance. Why she should require assistance when her jewellery had been returned and the supposed perpetrator had been apprehended, Zia had no idea. But Zia would've been glad of any kind of help or advice because she was feeling both sick and scared.

It went without saying that she had lost her job in the hotel where she had been working—not always legally—since she was fifteen as the owners were very friendly with Sandrine. Unhappily, she had no way of proving her innocence. Furthermore, if she was charged and arrested, a conviction for dishonesty could send her to prison and the resulting criminal record would destroy her future. She felt sick and alone and very, very scared.

When a swaggering older man arrived and urged the complaining guest straight across the fancy lobby into the traditional tea room on the other side, Zia relaxed infinitesimally, relieved to no longer be the target of the woman's accusing, angry stare.

The manager called her in and dismissed her, deaf to her pleas that she was being falsely accused. As she returned to the waiting area the older man reappeared alone and strode into the office she had just vacated to address the manager. A moment later, she was again called into the office as the manager departed.

'I'm Mr Caccia from the Mandovian Embassy here in London,' he informed her in a surprisingly upbeat tone. 'Your manager has loaned me his office so that I can speak to you in private, Your Highness.'

Her frown evaporated in her surprise as she glanced up, amazed to be addressed by that title.

'Of course, I know who you are,' he told her with wry amusement. 'And Mandovians definitely don't want to be embarrassed by reading in the newspapers that their Princess has been arrested for theft. This is a sensitive time in Mandovia with the reunification imminent. I have a proposal to make to you and I can see that you need practical help.'

Her frown line pleated her brows afresh. 'I don't understand.'

'I can protect you from a criminal charge of theft and bury this whole unsavoury matter,' he informed her. 'But in return you would have to come out to Mandovia for at least six months—'

'That's impossible for me—'

'You would be generously paid for your time there and comfortably housed, all of your needs met,' he assured her. 'You would have to attend events on our behalf, tour Upper Mandovia to be seen and to engage with your people. That may seem challenging to you but you would be richly rewarded for meeting those expectations. What do you think?'

'I think you're crazy,' Zia said weakly. 'I'm only a princess by birth and I don't know how to behave like one. While I would love to visit Mandovia some day, I have responsibilities here in London—'

'An elderly woman and a small dog. Yes, we know everything there is to know about you, Your Highness, including the education you have been diligently pursuing. The woman and the dog may accompany you to Mandovia. Obviously, your education could be deferred and continued at a later date. With the benefit of better financial resources, life would be much easier for you than it is at present—'

'Yes…but…' Zia's head was swimming at the sheer extent of the sweeping changes he was offering her. She would give her right arm, literally, to break their dependency on Sandrine and the grind of almost-round-the-clock labour. 'I would be paid for my time? And there would be accommodation included too?' she double-checked in wonderment.

'Yes,' he confirmed. 'My offer, which is official and courtesy of the Mandovian government, would provide you with a means of escape from your current trying circumstances below Sandrine Beccari's roof. Think about that fact and the possibilities. Right now, you are in serious trouble…and only I can make the trouble go away,' he completed smoothly.

'We don't even have passports,' she muttered.

'But you hold dual citizenship and the old lady is Mandovian as well. The embassy can immediately remedy the passport problem. However, the arrangements will take a couple of days to put in place,' he warned her. 'Meanwhile you can begin packing and preparing for your stay in Mandovia.'

Orazio froze as the prime minister strode into his office, ushered in by Harvey. Immediately rising from his desk, he strode forward to greet him, wondering why he was smiling broadly from ear to ear.

'Mr Milano.'

'Thank you for seeing me at such short notice,' the older man responded, taking a seat, smiling again as an employee appeared with a tray of coffee and biscuits. 'I'm the bringer of excellent news and I couldn't wait to tell you what Massimo Caccia has contrived to achieve in London for us. Princess Annunziata will be arriving in Mandovia within forty-eight hours—'

'How on earth did he achieve that?' Orazio enquired in frank astonishment.

'Massimo doesn't believe she ever received our official invitation or even knew of our interest. Apparently she lives in the basement of the London house in self-contained accommodation,' Bruno Milano revealed. 'He suspects her ex-guardian may have intercepted our communications for some nefarious reason of her own. According to Massimo, the young woman is delighted to agree to a six-month visit to Mandovia.'

Orazio nodded. 'That is, indeed, good news. But what are you planning to do with her for six months?'

'Actually…' the older man looked rather uncomfortable '…I was hoping that you would agree to host her here at the castle and teach her how to be royal.'

Orazio was aghast at that suggestion and it was a struggle to conceal his reaction. 'Having her here at the castle with me would stoke the royal marriage hopes,' he pointed out, tensing at that prospect. 'And between the staff and the number of visitors we receive, she would have no privacy. I'm also unsure that I could teach anyone how to be royal. She will require tutors in etiquette, history and PR before she can deal with the public in an appropriate way. Does she even still speak Italian?'

'Fluently, I understand. I must admit we didn't think of the privacy aspect—'

'And it would damage her status if someone was to talk to the press and reveal the mistakes that she will inevitably make. Her return will create so much excitement and curiosity that photos of her will be stolen and conversations recorded. If she's not up to immediate public exposure—'

'How *could* she be? Working as a chambermaid!' the older man exclaimed in dismay.

'Then we require a more discreet location for her to learn what she needs to know without an audience,' Orazio murmured, content to have made his point while frantically thinking of where a new princess could be stashed and tutored in the necessary skills without causing him any further annoyance.

And then the answer came to him and his dazzling smile flashed across his lean, bronzed features. 'I have the perfect place for her. My yacht, *Sea Empress*, currently moored in Türkiye. We can fly in the tutors. She'll need a wardrobe of suitable clothing as well—'

'Your yacht?' Bruno Milano was taken aback but relieved at the prospect of not having an unknown princess under siege from the paparazzi at the royal castle with an unwilling host. 'The government will cover all her expenses and that includes a salary—'

'A…*salary*?' Orazio repeated incredulously.

'She is very poor, Your Majesty. As Massimo acknowledges, she has to think of her future and being a princess needs to be a paying proposition for her to come here and stay for a while,' the older man clarified.

Gold-digger, Orazio decided on the spot, it being impossible for him to imagine being paid for what he saw as his duty. But he had also seen enough poverty to know that he was being unfairly prejudiced and he was quick to squash that label for the Princess in his head. Why shouldn't she be paid to fulfil the expectations of others? By all accounts, her life to date had been no fairy tale.

Zia lay in her bed in the basement apartment, sleepless and contemplating the changes on her horizon. She couldn't begin to imagine living in Mandovia, even if it would only be for six months. It was impossible to picture what she had never seen or a lifestyle she had never experienced. The concept of staying in a royal castle was simply intimidating. And she was quite sure King Orazio wouldn't be keen on that suggestion.

Why should he be? Royal to the backbone and richer than the legendary Midas, why would he want to house a fake princess such as she could only be? After all, what did she have going for her? Her late mother had been born a royal but only in a peripheral way because her Eastern European family had already been deposed royals without a throne. And from what Zia had established from the history books, her unlucky mother had been literally sold into marriage to a man old enough to be her father. A hated dictator, who had fancied having a real-life princess as a wife, believing she would add gloss and gravitas to his image.

So, for Zia, the immediate future was hugely scary and full of unknowns. But it was also the *escape* she had long sought from a life pinned and trapped beneath Sandrine's controlling thumb. At the end of the day, Zia reasoned, it didn't matter how frightening her new life would be in Mandovia. She would do it because she *had* to do it and had no other choice available. All her life to date had been like that and she was accustomed to taking the rough with the smooth.

But Orazio Arcangeli wouldn't want anything to do with her. She knew that, accepted it, still remembered him at the age of ten. Impossibly tall, very blond, aristocratic. Something about his measured way of speaking, his incredibly good manners and immense control even at that age had set her off into a tantrum. And Orazio had been stunned that a little girl would dare to fight him and possess such a temper. It made her laugh to know that their fathers had actually toyed with the ridiculous idea of marrying them off.

And she would bet what little cash she had that Orazio would *still* not be laughing about that stupid betrothal idea because Orazio was very serious in nature. If he wanted to marry a princess, she would be the very last one he would choose.

CHAPTER TWO

'The King will *personally* greet you on his yacht,' Massimo Caccia informed her with a huge smile of approval.

Still grappling with the news that she was not yet deemed fit for an immediate arrival in the country of her birth, Zia forced a smile in response. 'I don't want to put anyone out. It was very generous of him to allow us onto his yacht.'

'It wasn't generous,' Massimo contradicted. 'It was sensible. You have to learn so much before we can roll you out as a princess and His Majesty understands that better than anyone. It'll be like being sent back to school.'

Zia's smile set on her full lips. She wasn't some ignorant country girl requiring refinement and education and she would refuse to be treated like one by a condescending, ridiculously privileged Orazio. New clothing, yes, that would be a necessity, she conceded grudgingly. But my goodness, was she glad she had contrived to kick him when he was a boy because she had to be better behaved now that she was an adult.

The helicopter took off, making further conversation impossible, and Zia was relieved because Massimo Caccia had spent the whole flight from London bigging up Orazio in every way possible. In fact Massimo seemed to be the King's biggest fanboy. And Zia wasn't stupid, she had got the underwritten message of hope: people would love it if she married the very much single King. Immediately she had grasped why Orazio had switched her dose of 'princess school' from his royal home in the capital, Kyrene, to his yacht. Orazio didn't want to encourage false hopes. Orazio wanted a more hands-off role. Orazio didn't want to marry her either. And that was fine with her.

'Look at the yacht!' Massimo shouted in excitement as the helicopter made a stomach-churning turn before coming in to descend over the *Sea Empress*. 'My word, it's impressive!'

A shriek escaped Alina, who was a very nervous passenger. Zia patted her thin shoulder in reassurance and looked out of the window at the huge glistening silver-grey yacht that was anchored in the Bay of Marmaris. It was vast, more like a cruise ship than a privately owned vessel. The helicopter touched down on the helipad and Zia immediately rose to assist Alina, but Massimo was already helping the older woman with her belt and taking charge. He seemed to be, at heart, a kind man, she thought wryly, if somewhat abrupt and strident in manner.

Accepting a crewman's extended hand to steady her, Zia jumped out and the very first person she saw was Orazio, the *King*. Heaven knew he was gorgeous, all six feet four inches of him in height, not to mention his lean, muscular physique. Add the features of a Grecian god to that advantage and caramel-blond hair that gleamed pure gold in the Turkish sunshine and you had a male likely to attract attention everywhere he went. And that was even before you added in the wealth, the aura of power and authority and the title, she conceded.

Orazio stepped forward, brilliant green eyes welded to her. Yes, the Princess would need work and attention. She wore jeans, a tee shirt and scuffed canvas shoes and she was still absolutely tiny. Even so she was undeniably beautiful, from her mane of long blue-black gleaming hair loose round her slight shoulders to her perfect oval face dominated by blue eyes so deep a shade they carried a hint of violet. A delicate little nose in combination with a luscious pink mouth completed her features. He hadn't expected such a beauty and he stared in search of a flaw and lowered his lashes when he failed to find one, faint colour edging his strong cheekbones.

'Orazio…' she began uncertainly.

'That's too familiar a way to address the King,' Massimo chipped in unhelpfully from behind her, plunging her into embarrassment.

'Nonsense,' Orazio said easily. 'We have met before. Annunziata and I don't need to stand on ceremony on board the yacht.'

'Well, that's just as well,' Zia answered, making a fast recovery. 'Because I didn't know what to call you, nor do I know how to curtsy.'

'That is the sort of thing you will learn before you return to Mandovia but we only practise such habits at formal events,' he explained. 'My friends call me Raz, and I hope we will be friends.'

'I'm called Zia,' she said lightly. 'Even my mother

called me Zia. Annunziata is such a mouthful. I think the long string of names I was christened with was my father's choice.'

'Best not to mention the dictator,' Massimo slotted in.

'I won't mention him very often,' Zia replied calmly, 'but I can't pretend he didn't exist.'

'No, of course she can't,' Orazio commented, shooting a quelling look at the older man and turning to greet Alina, who was leaning on her walking stick and visibly uncomfortable to find herself in such lofty company.

A crew member came to escort the former nursemaid indoors to a seat and a promise of tea.

'I'll leave you here in safe hands,' Massimo said cheerfully and reached for Zia's hand to shake it. And with that he swung himself with some difficulty back into the helicopter to await his departure.

'I didn't realise he'd be leaving straight away,' Zia exclaimed in disappointment, because the older man had become familiar to her as a guide.

'I believe he is keen to get back to work,' Orazio commented, feeling a little guilty that he had not invited the older man to at least spend the night on board. He was aware that he had been rude, allowing personal feelings to come between him and common courtesy. In a sudden move he strode forward to advance the belated invitation, but he was waved back for safety reasons because the pilot was already preparing to take off.

Frustrated, Orazio retreated to lower a guiding hand to Zia's elbow as a door was held open for their entrance. 'I'm sure you're ready for a break from the travelling.'

'Not really,' she admitted. 'I've never travelled before. I don't remember arriving in the UK when I was a kid, so today has kind of been exciting for me.'

'A novel outlook.'

'Well, there's no point me pretending that I'm a seasoned anything really, because Massimo told me that everybody already knows that I was working as a chambermaid in London.'

'Yes, a Mandovian journalist reported that fact in our leading newspaper a few months ago and it caused a great deal of shock.'

'I can't think why. There's no shame in making an honest living. And the hours suited me, left me free to attend classes and look after...other things,' she muttered, falling silent, not wishing to mention Sandrine's demands. Already even thinking about their years of servitude to a vile, spoilt socialite made her so angry that she now wanted to explode. She had had to escape to feel safe enough to recognise that angry resentment.

In the imposingly large saloon furnished like a palatial drawing room, Alina was already pulling herself out of her armchair to say that she would like to lie down for a while. A stewardess in a smart uniform stepped forward and offered to take her to her cabin.

'Do you want me to come with you?' Zia asked.

'No...no, let someone else take care of me for a change,' Alina whispered urgently, her attention roving to Orazio and skittering nervously away again.

Reluctantly, Zia stayed where she was, recognising that Alina was too ill at ease to relax around a royal.

Orazio indicated a seat, shifted an imperious hand to order refreshments and waited for her to sit before settling opposite her. 'I'm glad you're used to taking classes. That'll make your stay on board more relaxed, although I imagine that you will find much of what you have to learn here very boring.'

'What do I have to learn?' Zia asked bluntly. 'Aside from curtsies and how to address important people?'

'Mandovian history.'

'I probably know as much about Mandovian history as you do.'

Orazio shot her an incredulous glance. 'I seriously doubt that.'

Zia tilted her chin in the kind of challenging response that Orazio was not accustomed to receiving from women. 'Ask me anything,' she invited. 'I'm good with your family tree back to your great-great-grandfather and my own family tree back to when my mother's ancestors still sat on a throne.'

'There's more to Mandovian history than family trees,' Orazio scoffed, taken aback by both the invitation and that level of information.

'So, ask your questions. Don't treat me as though I'm stupid.'

'I wasn't aware that I was doing that,' Orazio breathed deflatingly. 'It's childish to ask me to quiz you like a schoolgirl.'

'I don't think it is,' Zia disagreed. 'It would be a waste of time and money to pay someone to teach me what I already know!'

Totally self-possessed, Zia indicated a preference for coffee as she was offered a choice by the stewardess. Orazio studied her in growing frustration. He had never dealt with a woman less impressed by him or his status and it was strangely unsettling. He watched her sip her coffee utterly unconcerned by his frown, noted the stubborn angle of her chin, the fiery glint in her gorgeous eyes. Yes, damn his masculine brain for asserting that truth. Those eyes of hers set into that pale porcelain face currently a little pink with her annoyance were beautiful.

'Very well,' Orazio caved for the sake of peace and shot a question at her about the revolution almost twenty years before.

She answered it. When he dared to expand on her answer, she contradicted him with another point of view, reasoning that the Upper Mandovians viewed the revolution through a different prism from the Lower Mandovians, who had felt threatened by a virtual war of lawlessness erupting just over the border.

Challenged, Orazio went back further in history and she got every question right. 'OK,' he declared with rather bad grace. 'We'll scratch the history teacher from your schedule. Where did you learn so much history?'

'From books and newspapers at the library. I took an interest in Mandovia from quite a young age. It was something to cling to back then. Who I was, where I was from, *what* I was from.' Zia lifted a biscuit and crunched through it in the brooding silence. 'You did assume that I was going to be thick as a brick.'

'Of course, I didn't!' Orazio shot back at her. 'If you must know, working off our one and only meeting as children, I thought you would be a bad-tempered little shrew.'

Zia appreciated that honesty and nodded slowly. 'Oh,

I am…if you rub me up the wrong way, but it takes a lot to rile me. Unfortunately, you do it quite easily. You're so sure you know best, so certain of yourself… it's very annoying.'

'I'm not about to apologise.' Perfect white teeth flashed in a half-smile. For a split second, Orazio looked so stunningly handsome that she couldn't take her eyes off him. Those amazingly bright green eyes, that astonishing chiselled bone structure, the fine dark brows and lush black curling lashes. Anyone else with that shade of blond hair would have inherited blond or sandy brows and lashes, but Orazio had naturally got black to accentuate his already very striking eyes.

'You can relax with me, Orazio. I don't want to marry you either,' Zia told him boldly, amused by the way he froze in surprise at her frankness. 'I don't want to be a queen any more than I really want to be a princess, but agreeing to become a princess was my way out of a difficult situation. I will do my best with these classes but don't waste time having someone teach me about what cutlery I should use at the dinner table—I was a silver waitress as a teenager and I know cutlery and table manners backwards, forwards and sideways.'

'Another class will be struck from your timetable,' Orazio informed her with unholy amusement. 'You are a minx, Your Highness. Be aware that a woman has never told me before that she doesn't want to marry me.'

'I thought candour might let you relax a little more. After all, Massimo didn't conceal his fond hopes very well during the flight. Have you ever asked a woman to marry you?' she prompted with intense curiosity.

Faint colour outlined the model-like cheekbones that gave his lean, bronzed features such stunning impact. 'No.'

'But I imagine you have a lot of pressure on you to find a wife and start playing happy families,' she guessed with a grimace. 'Luckily for me, I'm just a surplus princess and unimportant in the grand scheme of the Mandovian reunification.'

'That's completely untrue. The people from your part of the country were extremely attached to your mother and revere her memory.'

'Yes, I've read that but, sadly for them, I'm not her. And I think if I'd had her life I would have started the revolution myself,' she admitted truthfully.

Orazio caught himself back on a helpless bout of appreciative laughter and studied her with frowning force. 'You can't say stuff like that in Mandovia. Someone would take offence and neither of us are supposed to express any opinion that sounds even slightly political.'

'Massimo already warned me of those boundaries. But surely I can say what I like to you?'

Orazio thought about that before releasing his breath in a slow hiss. 'Yes, you can.'

It occurred to him that Zia would become part of a very tiny minority in his life. He only ever spoke his mind freely to Fiero and his fiancée or his own grandfather. Very few people could be trusted to keep his opinions private and he would watch Zia carefully before he gave her that amount of trust. Her habit of saying exactly what she believed could be a disaster in the wrong situation and a PR nightmare. But he was surprised by the thought that it would be a shame to see such forthright speech silenced by royal convention.

She was very much an individual and she was totally unimpressed by his status. He had never met with such a reception before, particularly not from a young, attractive woman. He was infinitely better acquainted with being met with flattery and flirtation. She had argued with him, gone toe to toe with him, made an excellent point while discussing the revolution, a point he should've seen for himself. She was highly intelligent, quick on the draw...oddly fascinating, he conceded.

There was something very relaxing about a woman who told him upfront that she didn't want to marry him. Obviously she wasn't attracted to him. Why that should set his teeth on edge he had no idea as the news should've come as a relief. Was it because *he* found *her* attractive? He hadn't wanted to but he was a predictable male at heart and he did. She was bright, vivacious, outspoken and beautiful. He had never noticed that many positives in a woman before, even while acknowledging that the outspoken trait could be a dangerous weakness. In private, however, a male who lived in a world where so few spoke their minds or even told the truth, he found that candid trait uniquely captivating.

'So, what's she like?' Fiero asked immediately when he phoned his friend to bring him up to date.

'Different. Beautiful, opinionated, stubborn, clever, surprisingly well educated. Knows everything there is to know about Mandovia, including the news about the new National Park scheduled for the autumn,' Orazio told him.

'You sound like a guy with a crush.'

'And you're being weird again.'

'I've never heard you enthusing this way about a woman.'

'Oh, yes…she has no interest in marrying me,' Orazio imparted with enjoyment.

'And who raised that delicate subject?'

'*She* did. Massimo showed his hand during their time together and she cottoned on. She's not any keener on getting married than I am.'

'And yet I sense that you're offended,' his school friend commented. 'A princess without aspirations—'

'Evidently, and I *wasn't* offended,' Orazio swore.

'Tell that story to someone who hasn't known you practically from the day you were born,' Fiero quipped. 'Your lady friend in Paris is getting restless and phoned me to point out that you were supposed to be with *her* this weekend.'

'I was. I told her official business had come up.' Raz considered his current sexual partner without any sense of disappointment. Crystal was a gorgeous English fashion model and they had been intimate for a couple of months, which was pretty much the time limit on the extent of his interest. On his next visit he would be concluding that connection.

He tried to keep his sex life discreet but it was challenging to keep his name free of close female associations. If he spent more than ten minutes with any woman or laughed or smiled too often in her company, the rumours kicked off. It was embarrassing for the women involved when he had no serious intentions and so he met women out of the country, only had sex out of the country, only let loose outside Mandovia.

He functioned best with females who knew the relationship was going no further than the nearest bedroom. It was cold and transactional and against his deepest instincts, which craved the closeness, intimacy and emotion that had always been his ideal, particularly after the cold, distant childhood he had endured. It worked the best for him. An unemotional arrangement with a woman was safe, risked no scandals or tell-all confessions from ambitious wannabes and nobody got hurt. And that was just how his life had to work now. Strong moral standards were expected from him. He had learned that he wasn't allowed to be a young, single male with a healthy libido.

Upper Mandovia, at least, was a very conservative, God-fearing place and he had to maintain the illusion of being a clean-living monarch without inconvenient desires. Desires of a sexual nature were supposed to be met only within marriage. At the same time, however, nobody wanted him to turn into his father, who had married at a comparatively young age and had still continually sought out available women, which had triggered many ugly rumours. Orazio was conscious that he walked a tightrope of risk every time he visited that Parisian apartment. If that revelation ever hit the tabloids, he would be toast in the eyes of the most conservative Mandovians as proven to be a fake status symbol.

In truth, it would be easier for him to get married and settle down but he had a poor view of matrimony, raised by an essentially cold, embittered mother, who might as well have been a single parent even while still living with her lawfully wedded husband. He didn't want to risk marrying the wrong woman. He didn't feel any urge to settle down or have children. He thought he was still too young to make that life-changing decision.

'Dining with a king,' Alina mused, settling back into a chair in the corner of Zia's large, opulently furnished cabin. 'Whoever would've guessed you would be in this position?'

'Well, it never would have occurred to us even a week ago,' Zia sighed. 'He's less stuffy than I expected and more approachable.'

'He's very handsome,' Alina remarked with a smile.

Zia reddened. 'I don't think of him that way.'

'Be careful with him. You'll be alone with him at dinner. I asked for a tray in my room…and no, don't you try to argue with me. I'm staff…or retired staff,' the older woman muttered. 'I hope I know my place.'

'Your place is with me,' Zia replied, giving the older woman a fond hug before flipping open the built-in closet again and saying, 'The black or the red dress?'

'The red, you're too young to carry off black and, anyway, that was Sandrine's old frock.'

'So's the red,' Zia reminded her. 'But until I get new clothes, it's the best I've got.'

'The red's a little low-necked,' Alina opined in an uneasy undertone. 'You wore it for that Christmas staff party at the hotel but—'

'It'll do fine,' Zia cut in with decision. 'Gosh, I miss Sausage.'

'Yes, but he'll be waiting for us in Mandovia when we leave here,' Alina reminded her cheerfully. 'Apparently the King has two mastiffs at the castle. The stewardess told me that he rarely brings them here onto the yacht because of the quarantine restrictions.'

Zia set the red dress on the bed. A dog lover, was he? It was another point in his favour. As Alina returned to her cabin, she undressed for a shower, eager to freshen up after the long day and all the travelling and sitting around. Yet barely a week ago she had been unemployed and facing a charge of theft, she reminded herself, but the man from the embassy, Massimo Caccia, had made all that go away and had transformed her life.

Even so, it was only temporary, she reminded herself. She would have six months without any need to worry about bills and then she would be free to continue her life as she chose. She had never enjoyed such freedom. Alina, she suspected ruefully, would probably reunite with her widowed sister in Mandovia and could well decide to remain there in her home village with her only surviving family. Could she herself decide to stay on in Mandovia too?

She smoothed the red dress down over her hips. Alina had altered it to fit her after Sandrine had thrown it away because it had a cigarette burn in the skirt. The full swell of her bust at the neckline looked slightly racy to her critical gaze, but she couldn't help that because she was much larger in that department than its original owner had been. Short and curvy in both breast and hip, that was her shape and she was stuck with what she had been born with, regardless of how she had long envied Sandrine's tall, slender, elegant figure.

Orazio almost forgot himself and performed a double take when Zia entered the saloon. When she had worn her shapeless tee shirt and loose jeans he had had little idea of Zia's build. And now, here she was unveiled… *literally*! A glorious hourglass shape. It was a struggle not to let his gaze linger on the pale plump curves of her luscious breasts.

'What would you like to drink?' he asked as a steward hovered by the bar in readiness.

'May I have a cocktail?' Zia asked. 'I've never had one but I would love to try one.'

'A Mojito,' Orazio ordered on her behalf. 'So, you drink alcohol?'

'Yes. It doesn't have much effect on me though,' Zia told him truthfully. 'I've had drinks with work and classmates and it's never affected me. I could probably drink you under the table.'

Orazio laughed at that far-reaching display of confidence. 'Well, we won't be having a competition tonight.'

He was touched by her honesty and slightly unnerved by it as well. There was a dangerous naivety about her and he could see such an attribute making her vulnerable to a certain type of man. Not that that was any of his business, but it would do her no harm to become a little more worldly-wise before she went out to be a princess in public.

'Tell me about your childhood with Sandrine Beccari,' Orazio prompted over the dinner table thirty minutes later, when Zia was embarking on her second Mojito and contemplating the beautiful meal in front of her. 'I was surprised that she kept you with her because you have an uncle and an aunt on your mother's side.'

Zia lost visible colour and she dealt him an uneasy glance before stiffening her facial muscles. 'Oh, she tried to pass me off onto them once she realised my parents were dead, but my mother's relatives weren't interested…the orphan daughter of a hated dictator? No, they weren't prepared to take me on. Sandrine ensured that I knew that I was just an embarrassment to them. It might have been different had I come with money, but I was penniless.'

'But you were never penniless,' Orazio reasoned with conviction. 'That house in London belonged to your mother and it was your inheritance. How else could you have lived there?'

And shock at that bold statement settled over Zia like an enveloping fog. The idea that that house had actually belonged to her from the moment of her mother's passing shook her inside out. 'I always believed that the house belonged to Sandrine. I mean, I knew that she didn't pay rent or a mortgage, but I always *assumed*—'

'No, that house is yours by right of inheritance…unless your mother signed it over to the Beccari woman before she passed,' he conceded.

Zia's lashes fluttered in bewilderment. 'I wouldn't have thought that there was time for that the night we left Mandovia but that would finally explain to me why she kept Alina and me with her. It would've meant that she had the use of free accommodation in London,' she registered slowly.

'There was also a trust set up with the purchase of the house that should've taken care of most of the bills,' Orazio volunteered. 'I believe your mother foresaw the fall of your father's regime and set up a safe harbour in London for you both…only you appear not to have managed to benefit from what was rightfully yours.'

Pale as milk, Zia asked for another Mojito to replace her empty glass and Orazio summoned the server to fulfil her request. She couldn't believe what she was being told, that she had not been the penniless orphan housed and raised by her guardian who had taken pity on her. Instead, it seemed as though Sandrine had taken advantage of *her* to seize possession of the house that legitimately belonged to her charge. Deep anger rippled through Zia as she looked back on the life she had lived, always made to feel like a charity case and a burden, denied her freedom and her education while being constantly threatened if she protested or failed to toe the line. She took a deep swig of her refreshed cocktail.

'It seems I've been had and no mistake,' she pronounced flatly. 'I've never met with a solicitor. I wasn't aware that I had an inheritance of any kind.'

'I can put my legal team onto investigating what happened,' Orazio proffered.

'I would appreciate that,' she said quietly.

'I suspect that you've been ripped off too.'

'Very probably,' Zia acknowledged. 'I would be grateful if that was sorted out for me. The real problem when I was a child was that there was nobody around to oversee Sandrine's guardianship. She kept me because nobody else was willing or available to take care of me.'

'That was wrong,' Orazio conceded. 'I think you fell through the cracks. Upper Mandovia was so grateful to be free of your father's regime that they took no interest in what happened to his surviving child—'

'Until *now*...' Zia chipped in with a raw emphasis that pulled at something deep in his chest. 'When suddenly there *is* a use for me, a *reason* for me to exist because of my mother's legacy. And yet I'm not remotely like her. She was a yes-woman with her family and with my father, doing exactly what she was told, never thinking there might be something better out there. I'm not like that. My life has toughened me up and made me want more.'

Involuntarily entrapped by the raw emotions flickering across her expressive face, Orazio prompted, 'Why was it so tough?'

'Sandrine was cruel. I'll be fair. When she got me, I was a spoilt three-year-old and probably difficult but she thumped and kicked me into obedience. And if I didn't bow down quickly enough, she took her rage out on Alina instead,' she confided shakily, recalling past episodes that had deeply upset her. 'I couldn't stand to see Alina punched to the ground, so I gave in. And Sandrine made me into an unpaid servant. As Alina grew more frail, I had to do her job, and I was put to work in the hotel kitchens at fifteen because Sandrine was friendly with the owners and she said I needed the discipline. But in reality, she just wanted more money because I never saw any of it—'

'And your education?' Orazio probed, very much shocked by what she was telling him. 'What happened with that?'

'Sandrine insisted that I was being homeschooled and Alina wasn't capable of teaching me anything beyond the basics. I knew I couldn't get us away from Sandrine without a decent job, so my focus was on educating myself, going to college, becoming a teacher—'

'A modest goal for a princess,' Orazio commented.

'Oh, for goodness' sake,' she exclaimed as a delicious

creamy dessert was set before her. 'I've never been a princess except on paper. You've been a prince since the day you were born and raised with all that stuff. But it's foreign territory for me.'

'But it shouldn't have been.' Brilliant green eyes assailed and held hers fast across the table. 'I'm very sorry that that has been your experience and I can only hope that your time in Mandovia will allow you to believe that you *are* important to our people and that you do have much to offer them.'

Zia shrugged, feeling the quickened beat of her heart thudding away like a runaway train inside her, a little mortified at how the rasp of his deep-pitched voice and his intense appraisal unleashed reactions that were far too new for her to feel comfortable with. Yes, Orazio was drop-dead gorgeous, but he was as far removed from her as the moon. He was so intense. When he studied her the way he had been doing, gooseflesh lifted on her bare arms and heat surged through her in a way that made her tense. As a rule men left her cold. She had been through all the usual teenaged experiences while attending night classes and working at the hotel and not a single kiss or a disappointment from a guy had prepared her for a male of Orazio's cut. Sleek, sophisticated, poised and shockingly calm in comparison to her more volcanic temperament.

'That's kind of you to say,' she replied as levelly as she could manage.

'I'm appalled by what you have endured,' Orazio admitted tautly. 'It was unconscionable that nobody thought to check on your well-being, particularly when you were in that woman's charge and at her mercy.'

'Yet she was my mother's best friend,' Zia reminded him wryly.

Frowning, Orazio straightened his broad shoulders. 'She was also a salaried attendant and your father's mistress.'

Yet another wallop of shock bowled through Zia and she trembled in receipt of it. She wanted to question his statement but she remembered the almost personalised hatred Sandrine had always seemed to have for her and, all of a sudden, so much of the older woman's resentment of her existence made better sense. She breathed in slow and deep and pushed away her untouched dessert, her appetite having vanished.

'You didn't *know*?' Orazio demanded in surprise.

'How could I have known such a thing? Yes, I read books that hinted that my father wasn't faithful to my mother, but there was never any proof or any names. I had no reason to suspect that someone as trusted as Sandrine was in our home could've been secretly involved with him. Obviously, my mother *didn't* know,' Zia said flatly. 'If she *had* known, she would never have given me to her and trusted her to take me to safety. My mother had complete faith in her. I could never understand why Sandrine acted as she did until now, when I suppose she felt she had stronger reasons to resent me and make my life miserable—'

'I've given you far too many unpleasant surprises for one evening,' Orazio registered, reading her pale, troubled face without difficulty.

'Since what you know appears to be common knowledge, I prefer to know those facts now. I don't want to be told anything sugar-coated or false,' she told him valiantly.

'We'll have coffee out on deck,' he suggested, gesturing to the hovering server with an ease that told her that he had lived with staff all his life. He barely had to speak to have his needs met. It was humbling and reminded her just how far she had stepped out of her own much more workaday milieu.

They moved onto a beautifully furnished outside deck with soft lights that was set into an alcove for privacy. She poured the coffee into the delicate china cups. 'You live in a different world,' she complained.

'It's your world as well.'

'No, I'm just a temporary visitor,' Zia scoffed without hesitation.

'That is *not* how you should feel. You were born in Mandovia,' he reminded her.

'But I barely remember my life there,' she traded.

'That doesn't matter,' Orazio insisted.

Zia sipped her coffee, her head swimming a little as she did so, making her think that that last cocktail might not have been the best idea. Maybe she hadn't eaten enough to balance out the alcohol. The shocks Orazio had dealt her had blitzed her brain and now she was so tired she simply wanted to lie down and sleep.

'I want to go to bed,' she murmured, setting down her empty cup, suddenly aware that she had slurred her words. 'I think I'm tipsy.'

'That's my fault,' Orazio told her, rising fluidly to his feet. 'I shouldn't have paid heed to your claims. Perhaps what you drank before had a low-alcohol content.'

'Who knows?' Zia quipped, standing up and swaying slightly.

'I'll see you back to your room.' Planting a steadying arm to her spine, Orazio urged her back indoors.

'There's no need. I can find my own way,' she mumbled, feeling dizzy.

Orazio ignored her words, cursing himself for being so careless with her well-being. He didn't want anyone on board to notice the condition she was in because it would create talk that would not be flattering to her image.

'Everything's going round and round. I don't like this,' she confided, momentarily resting the back of her head against his shoulder, drinking in the scent of him.

Her thoughts were all over the place. He smelt like forest trees on an icy night, she reflected abstractedly, crisp and vital and fresh. He walked her along an endless companionway, said a bad word under his breath as she stumbled and, when they reached the stairs, he simply swept her up off her feet and carried her up, up and up. He set her down again with care and finally opened a door a few feet further on.

'I'll go to bed,' she mumbled sleepily.

'Not until I know you'll be all right alone,' Orazio countered, pressing her over the threshold and following her in, firmly closing the door.

'Why wouldn't I be all right alone?' she framed dizzily.

Without a word he lifted her off her feet again and rested her down gently on top of the bed, slipping off her high heels in a deft motion and then easing her onto her side. 'Do you feel ill?' he asked.

'No, just tired.' She gazed up at him with very wide violet-blue eyes. 'You're smoking hot, Orazio—'

'Raz,' he corrected with precision, tamping down the satisfaction that blossomed at her compliment. 'Go to sleep.'

'Why do you always wear a tie?' she muttered critically, taking in his beautifully tailored suit and immaculate shirt.

'Because I'm never off duty—'

'You wear a tie with swimming trunks too?'

'Sleep...' Orazio told her in a low-pitched undertone.

'You sound like that snake in *Jungle Book*,' she sighed and her lashes dropped.

Orazio tossed the throw at the foot of the bed over her, hung around long enough to hear her breathing deepen and steady, and then listened at the door before sliding out and closing it behind him.

The sly, seductive *snake* in the cartoon? Well, thanks a lot for that comparison, Zia. Raking long, impatient fingers through his hair, he headed for his own bed, knowing that he wanted her but that he absolutely couldn't have her, not without a ring and all the pizzazz. He cursed himself for his own weakness. The attraction would burn out. For him, it always did. A few weeks from now, he would be treating her like anyone else around him, untouched by the deep ache of arousal currently afflicting him.

CHAPTER THREE

ZIA WOKE UP with a headache, still fully dressed, and groaned out loud, worried that she had made a fool of herself the night before. She had a burning, chafing memory of telling Raz that he was 'smoking hot'.

When she emerged from the shower and walked back into her cabin, a stewardess was waiting with a tray that bore a smoothie green drink and painkillers. Her stiff face folded into a reluctant grin as she recognised Raz's intervention and she accepted both offerings.

Breakfast was being served upstairs in the main saloon and she was meeting with a stylist and a tailor as soon as she had eaten. Princess school was kicking off, she acknowledged wryly. It would be fun to have new clothes but not if they tried to stick her in anything frilly or flouncy. Reckoning that there would be measurements taken, she put on a black skirt and a white shirt, rather than her usual denim.

Orazio was already at the dining table. 'How are you feeling?' he asked lightly.

'Surprisingly good…considering,' Zia told him. 'I think I said some things I shouldn't have said—'

'I didn't notice,' Raz assured her calmly. 'I was worried about you.'

'You were very kind,' she said awkwardly, warm colour flooding her oval face. 'I'm sorry I drank too much—'

'No. You learned some upsetting truths last night,' Orazio reminded her softly. 'And it was better for you to discover your alcohol limits with me rather than someone else. At least, you can trust me to act in your best interests.'

And bizarrely, Zia wanted to slap him for that assurance because she doubted there was a normal, breathing woman alive who wanted to be assured that Orazio was not remotely tempted by her attractions. He had set aside her appreciation and encouragement and even excused her forward behaviour as if she were a misbehaving adolescent rather than a grown-up. She gave him a bland smile and inwardly slapped herself for being so easily hurt. They weren't kids, they were adults, and he might not be attracted to her but she was hopelessly attracted to him and needed to keep that reality utterly to herself from now on.

Orazio breathed again only when her lashes dropped, concealing those strikingly beautiful eyes of hers. She wasn't easy to head off at the pass, as it were. And fortunately for him, as long as he remained seated, the tight fit of his tailored trousers was not noticeable, although it was becoming dangerously habitual for him to be aroused by her mere presence. Acknowledging the reciprocal attraction between them would only make things awkward since they were not free to act on it.

He had to treat her like a little sister, which was difficult when he was very much an only child.

How did she contrive to look so appealing even when she was dressed like a waitress? Those sexy curves at hip and breast drew him like a magnet, not to mention the coconut scent of her soft skin and the little breathy sounds she had made when he'd placed her on her bed. It was all wrong, not normal for him, at least *not* on home turf, and he had to suppress it or he might just end up like his mother: trapped in a bad marriage by pure sexual attraction alone.

'I'm returning to Mandovia this morning,' Orazio imparted, long fingers raking restively at his luxuriant hair to push it back from his brow.

'You're leaving?' she said in dismay.

'I'll be back in a couple of weeks and I'll phone you whenever I can—'

'I don't own a phone. I couldn't afford one.'

'That will be remedied today,' Orazio informed her. 'When I call, you can tell me what the tutoring is like,' he heard himself promise, taken aback by that instinctive urge to soothe her and make her happy.

'You'll ring?' she checked and her sunshine smile broke out, lighting up her beautiful face, and for a split second he couldn't look away.

'When you're finished learning, I'll take you out sightseeing as a break from all the boring stuff you'll have to learn this month.'

Twenty minutes later, she stood watching the helicopter disappear over the mountains in the distance and then her official day began. As she had expected, precise measurements were taken of her height and size and afterwards a stylist sat with her, trying to establish her preferences while continually reminding her that it was to be a traditionalist wardrobe, as if someone somewhere was terrified she would break out into microminiskirts and glittery dresses slashed to the navel. She picked clear, fresh colours and tailored garments, taken aback by how many different outfits had to be obtained. She was also to be provided with swimwear and leisure gear, not to mention undergarments and accessories.

That was followed by a session on the etiquette of greeting people according to their status and importance. Learning how to curtsy, as she was informed she ought to do the minute Orazio entered a room, gave her the giggles. According to the powers-that-be, he was the only person in Mandovia she would have to curtsy around and she was relieved, knowing that Raz wasn't about to be encouraging much of that kind of behaviour in his vicinity because nobody bowed or anything on his yacht.

'His Majesty doesn't like a fuss,' her tutor informed her, 'but it is wise to do what you should do in case you are being observed.'

The class that followed was devoted entirely to showing her pictures of dozens of Mandovians, all the VIPs from both sides of the country, it seemed, whom she would meet and need to identify, from the politicians to the local bigwigs and the celebrities. There were so many faces to recognise that she soon realised that that was where the real challenge of work would begin. She would have to memorise all those faces and learn to recognise them all within a couple of weeks.

Even so, she was seriously worried when she recognised the hotel guest who had accused her of theft in that long, confusing line-up of photos of important people. Sofia Marone was married to one of the richest men in Mandovia and what would happen if she recognised Zia as the maid she believed had tried to steal her diamond brooch? And why was Massimo Caccia, whom she had believed worked for the embassy in London, listed as a prominent government special advisor?

She would have to tell Orazio the truth about her sudden decision to visit Mandovia. She winced at the prospect. Massimo had warned her not to tell anyone about what had happened at the hotel, but she didn't see how she could avoid confiding in Orazio when there was a possibility that she could be introduced to the woman who believed she was a thief. That story would embarrass everybody, not least Zia, and it would provoke an ugly scandal. She dared not keep that experience to herself and hope for the best.

At lunchtime, she tracked down Alina, resting back on a lounger on deck while happily ensconced in a pile of glossy magazines that showed the famous, the great and the good and shared all the gossip about their lives in Mandovia. Zia listened as her former nursemaid burbled on about some of the well-known faces who had featured in her own lessons. Alina, evidently, was content on the yacht, delighted to have access to other Mandovians and the latest Mandovian soap operas on the television in her cabin. For the first time, Zia realised that Sandrine was now only a bad memory from the past.

She thought sadly of her poor mother entrusting her

only daughter to a woman who had been sleeping with her husband, and she was pained by the new hurtful truths that now coloured her life. But it was better to know reality than to remain in ignorance when there had to be others who knew the same facts. Possibly, though, Orazio as King knew more secrets than most about Zia's background.

The two women had packed up and vacated the basement flat while Sandrine was still in bed, so there had been no final confrontation: Sandrine never rose from bed before noon. That period of her life was over and done, Zia reminded herself, and if Raz kept his promise and asked his legal advisors to check out her supposed inheritance, she would eventually discover whether or not she *did* own the house in London. That would be important for the future, as six months in Mandovia would soon pass.

That afternoon, she met the PR team, who worked for Orazio at the royal castle outside Kyrene. Their task was to teach her how to gracefully sidestep awkward questions and to keep her face expressionless. She was assured that at any public occasion she attended she would have a PR person beside her, ready to prompt or direct her if necessary. Having been shown several car-crash interviews on a laptop as a demonstration of what not to say or do, Zia appreciated that she would be walking into a public minefield and would have to pick up the required skills as quickly as possible. It was daunting, she acknowledged, to be expected to learn in a few weeks the smooth expertise that Orazio had probably been honing from early childhood. She resolved to speak as little as possible to avoid the pitfalls and concentrate on polite, interested smiles instead. Better people assumed that she was stupid, rather than rude or tactless!

'Don't be so friendly,' she was gently reproved in an embarrassing mock-up of an ordinary conversation. 'Practice a little distance. You're a royal.'

But she wasn't a royal and never would be on Orazio's scale. His family had been on the throne for generations, acting, *real* royals in Mandovia with people bowing and curtsying around them and treating them like rare, refined jewels to be treasured. Her mother had been adored, perhaps because her acts of kindness, charity and compassion had stood out as such a contrast to her husband's brutal regime. But she hadn't been adored for the blood in her veins or deemed royal in the same way as Orazio Arcangeli. And Zia worried that if she seemed to act too high or fancy, people wouldn't take to her at all.

The next fortnight evaporated in a blur of endless memorising and clothes fittings. Garments came and went, returned for final fitting adjustments, and her wardrobe steadily expanded.

Most evenings, Raz phoned her, occasionally filling her in on his own routine but more often questioning her about what she was learning. She relaxed with him more with every phone call, grateful that she had someone in her life who understood the steep learning curve she was on.

Orazio landed back on the yacht three weeks later, accompanied by Fiero and his fiancée, Allegra, generally known as Allie to her friends.

His first view of Zia was long distance and she was in the pool being taught how to swim by his captain's first officer, Pietro. 'The Princess is a very quick learner. Once we realised that she was unable to swim, we knew that was a problem because naturally you will want to take her into the water,' the captain of the *Sea Empress* pointed out.

'Naturally,' Fiero mocked in Orazio's ear. 'Particularly if she's a five-foot-tall pocket Venus with the face of a Botticelli angel.'

'Enough!' Raz snapped in an undertone to his friend, who had ribbed him mercilessly throughout the previous week when he made a last-minute trip to Paris to conclude his arrangement with Crystal and then worked twice as hard as usual to free up his weekend to return to Türkiye. 'You're aware that I invited you and Allie to join us as chaperones.'

'Invite the old lady to join us. She'll be twice as effective as we could ever be. I don't think you've ever listened to my advice in your life,' Fiero sighed.

Orazio ignored him, picking up binoculars to spy on Zia's swimming lesson in the pool on the deck below. She wore a red costume that hugged her God-given, glorious curves like a glove and the tenor of his breathing roughened. He didn't like seeing another man's hands on her even in the water, even if the man involved was old enough to be her father and the parent of two teenaged daughters himself. His staff had been reporting back on her to him from the start. He had been told that she learned fast, had an excellent memory and also spoke reasonably good Spanish, which would be welcome news to the rural occupants of the mountains of

Upper Mandovia, which rejoiced in many families of Spanish extraction.

Zia was eager for the swimming lesson to conclude because she was very much aware that Orazio was back on board and she didn't want to greet him with wet hair and no make-up. Donning a towelling wrap, she thanked Pietro for teaching her and hastened back to her cabin, wondering who the guests were that Orazio had returned with. She raced into the shower, making full use of the excellent toiletries she now had at her disposal. Make-up too and right now she had more clothes than she had ever seen outside a big shop, reckoning that it would be hard to return to ordinary life after being plunged into such luxury.

It had been a long few weeks during which she had learned all sorts of new things. She could now walk in high heels, without looking down all the time afraid to trip, and with her head held high. She could put on make-up too, when previously she had only ever owned lipstick. Now, her heart thumping like a road drill inside her chest, she flipped through her newly extensive wardrobe and chose a blue cocktail frock to wear, tagged by a helpful PR lady as perfect for a dinner date. She wanted Orazio to see the change in her and appreciate the extent of the makeover that she had received. Even her hair had been expertly trimmed and styled so that it fell effortlessly into place.

Orazio dressed up more than he usually did for dinner because, helpfully, he had been informed that the Princess was dressing up. He agreed to eating the Princess's favourite dessert as well, as apparently the chef was one of her new fans. He also noticed that an inordinate number of the crew were hovering when he arrived in the saloon to join his guests for drinks. He hadn't realised that his very first meeting with Zia would be put under so much scrutiny and it unnerved him a little.

And then Zia arrived and performed the most perfect curtsy in the doorway in spite of her towering heels. He wanted to laugh at the formality but he knew she would be furious if he did, so his lean bronzed features merely stiffened as his attention raked over her, emerald-green eyes vibrant with interest. She walked towards him, all dignity abandoned as she chattered constantly.

'I knew you were back but I was in the pool and I didn't want to drip over you…and I wanted you to see how much better I look now, all gussied up like a fancy Christmas turkey for public consumption.' And she said all that without drawing breath and he was laughing and moving to greet her before he even knew what he was doing.

'You looked amazing before I left and now you simply look more amazing,' Orazio asserted, grasping her fluttering, uncertain hands and pulling her closer. *'Amazing,'* he repeated stubbornly, his gaze roaming over the shiny blue-black strands of hair framing her exquisite face, the brilliance of her bright eyes and the smile on her lush pink mouth. His eyes lingered there on the soft plump curve of her inviting lower lip and arousal skated through him in an unwelcome sizzle of awakening lust, making him step back.

Fiero cleared his throat to remind him that he had company.

'This is Fiero Cattaneo. My executive assistant, business manager, go-to for everything, best friend,' Raz introduced warmly. 'And Allegra Abate, his fiancée and soon to be his wife, always known as Allie—'

'We're getting hitched next month,' a tall, attractive blonde stepped forward to announce and Zia was pleased to notice that she herself was similarly clad. A fear of somehow getting something wrong seemed to cloud her every thought, she conceded ruefully, knowing that she would have to overcome that dread and learn to handle the mistakes she was certain to make.

The company was lively over the meal that followed and she relaxed. Straight away it was obvious to Zia that Orazio, Fiero and Allie were longstanding friends. Fiero and Allie had both had parents employed by or attached to the court and had been frequent visitors to the royal castle as children. Allie now ran an event-planning business that handled some of the formal occasions held at the castle.

Zia had only one glass of wine, sticking to water the rest of the time, mindful that she had to be careful in company. She ignored Orazio's attempts to pour her a second glass, irritated enough to glare at him the third time he tried to top up her glass. *'No!'* she said, louder than she had intended, seeing his hard jawline flex and tighten and belatedly aware that she had been too blunt again.

'Why not?' he demanded, infuriating her.

'You know why not,' she pointed out thinly.

He slanted her a glittering smile that made her heart skip a beat and flushed colour into her cheeks. 'But you were so cute,' he teased.

'I don't aspire to be cute,' Zia told him without hesitation. 'I'll be in Mandovia to perform a job and I intend to do it to the best of my ability. I can't afford to drink and let my guard down.'

'And that's me told,' Orazio quipped with amusement, gleaming green eyes roaming over her compressed lips and exasperated gaze.

'Unlike you, I won't be given a licence to be whoever I want to be. I'll be scrutinised and criticised and I won't make myself a target—'

'You're right,' Allie responded. 'I guess the PR team have been warning you of all the pitfalls of public life.'

Zia smiled and nodded, reclaiming her relaxation in receipt of that understanding. Orazio had become a much-wanted monarch because he had refused the throne when it was first offered to him, only surrendering once he realised how many people were eager for him to continue in the steps of his family predecessors. Nobody had warned him that one false step could condemn him in the eyes of all because everybody was aware that he had been raised to become King by his father and he'd already known the score.

'You shouldn't flirt with Zia either,' Fiero warned quietly. 'That will only encourage rumours.'

'I wasn't flirting with her.'

'You *were*,' Zia contradicted apologetically. 'Maybe it comes so naturally to you that you don't realise you're doing it.'

'I'll be more circumspect once we're back in Mandovia,' Orazio swore with pleasure. 'May I ask how you learned Spanish?'

'Alina speaks Spanish, Sandrine spoke Italian. I'm practically bilingual. It was English I struggled with when I first worked,' Zia parried, wondering when she would take the opportunity to tell him about that theft charge that she had suffered back in London. It wouldn't be over dinner with an audience, but perhaps when they went sightseeing she would get him alone for a few minutes. She would need to speak to him but she, certainly, wasn't looking forward to it. Suppose that he didn't believe that she *was* innocent? Suppose that he suspected that she *was* an actual thief?

She watched Orazio chatting. He truly was a devastatingly handsome male, the blonder strands in his caramel hair glinting pure gold below the lights, his green eyes framed by lush black lashes twinkling with amusement, his mouth curling into his easy grin. Feeling her skin heat beneath Allie's steady scrutiny, she turned her head away, not wanting her attraction to Orazio to be obvious. A little while later, she faked a yawn and said it was time for her to turn in, especially as Orazio had mentioned a very early departure in the morning.

Comfortably clad in linen cropped trousers and a vintage band shirt of her own teamed with trainers, Zia had a light breakfast in her cabin and joined the others in the saloon in perfect time to troop down to the launch that would take them to shore. Orazio looked almost unrecognisable in a baseball cap, a loose white linen shirt and khaki chinos. Accompanied by a four-strong security presence, they climbed into an air-conditioned luxury people-carrier and got on the road. In the hills they climbed a rough track up to the early city of Amos and saw the watchtowers and the city gates before standing on the cliffs to admire the view of Kumlubuk Bay and the silvery olive groves surrounding them.

'I'm not very fit,' Zia said, still out of breath from the climb.

'You'll get there.'

'You're not even out of breath,' she complained.

'I'm in the gym at five every morning for a workout,' Raz murmured with amusement. 'It's my routine and the only way I keep up.'

They broke the drive in a village where they sat under an ancient plane tree and drank cold apple tea. And then it was on to Ephesus in the baking heat, their guide awaiting them at the entrance and accompanying them, showing them the points of interest. Orazio, naturally, had visited it all before and answered her every question as they wandered round the Great Theatre where St Paul had once preached.

After that visit, they arrived at the hotel in the mountains and it was a revelation for Zia. She had never seen a property that rejoiced in that level of opulence before—no, not even after working for years in an exclusive London hotel. They were ushered to their suites like the most important visitors on the planet.

'Well, you are,' Allie pointed out in a helpful aside. 'This place belongs to Raz. He has many diversified interests and this hotel is his and used only by VIPs. We're being treated to a fabulous spa session here too this evening. I've been here once before as his guest and I absolutely loved it.'

They dined in the owners' suite before Zia and Allie returned to their rooms to don towelling robes and swimsuits for the spa in the basement. There they were plunged into the kind of immersive experience that Zia had never had before. A Turkish bath complete with soaping and pummelling and massaging was the first step, followed by waxing, which Zia was less keen on but which Allie cajoled her into tolerating. Every treatment available in the beauty sphere was on offer but Zia had already been through endless beauty sessions on the yacht and the concept of hair oils and head massages now left her cold. Been there. Done that, didn't long for it again, particularly not after the waxing repeat.

Leaving the blonde to her luxury hair experience, she walked down the stairs into the basement bathing pools and was instantly filled with wonder at the seemingly natural beauty of her surroundings. They were modelled on Roman baths and built in genuine caves but decorated with contemporary tastes in mind, glowing lights softly illuminating secluded alcoves while water streamed down over marble walls. It was atmospheric and magical and she descended the steps into the thermal heat of the water with a breathy sigh of pleasure, feeling the heat of the day and the tiredness of all the activity drop away from her.

Orazio watched her emerge from the shadows and his jawline clenched. He didn't need to see the Princess in a bathing costume that highlighted every magnificent curve of her perfect hourglass figure. He had endured a long day, striving not to flirt or react in any specific way to the Princess of Upper Mandovia. Fiero had warned him off but Allie had been even more blunt. 'Don't play with her,' his friend's fiancée had warned him. 'She's not one of your amoral yes beauty queens. I don't think she's very sophisticated. Keep your distance because you *can't* have a fling with her.'

Solid good sense but, in truth, Princess Annunziata

should've come with a health warning, Raz reckoned, because he found her unbelievably tempting. She was pretty as a picture and utterly unspoiled, noticeably different from the type of women with whom Raz usually amused himself. That natural quality and her lively personality drew him, even though he knew he shouldn't be reacting that way. Her honesty was even more hugely attractive to a male unaccustomed to receiving candour from any woman, up to and including his own mother, who had always lied when it had suited her to do so. He wasn't ready to get married yet, but Zia was absolutely the type of woman a man married. A for-ever kind of woman, he reflected uneasily.

'Raz…' Zia muttered, taken aback by his appearance and his half-naked state, a pair of swim shorts hanging low on his lean hips showcasing an eight-pack torso that would not have looked out of place on a Hollywood movie star. She was dumbstruck, staring, watching water droplets roll down his hard muscular pecs, noticing the furrow of dark golden hair leading down over his flat stomach to disappear into the waistband of his shorts and the masculine fullness lower down. Her mouth ran dry, her breathing shortening in her tight lungs. 'I didn't know you were down here.'

'It's been a long, hot day. I didn't think I could sleep without a dip to cool off,' he murmured smoothly, watching water bead across the pillowy slopes of her full breasts in what was undeniably a very modest suit but which her wonderful shape overfilled in the best way possible. His desire, his immediate urge to touch, was instantaneous. It was not at all what he wanted to feel, but that he felt it and that his body was reacting regardless were indisputable facts.

'Allie is getting some fancy hair treatment. I'd had enough fluffing and fussing, so I left her to it,' Zia advanced awkwardly, positively affronted to find herself on full display in a figure-hugging swimsuit in front of Orazio, because the water at that point only washed to her thighs and exposed all the parts of her figure that embarrassed her: the bountiful breasts, the full hips, the meaty thighs. Raised in the vicinity of Sandrine, who had about as many curves as a sheet of cardboard, Zia had very set ideas about what made a woman attractive and fanciable to the male sex. A casual boyfriend who had suggested that a diet would be a good idea hadn't helped her self-image.

'Not a fan of spas?' Raz quipped.

'Never been to a spa until today but the major makeover on your yacht was *enough*,' she stressed with a slight wince. 'Primping and preening to this extent wouldn't be an interest for me, but I could see that Allie was having a whale of a time and I didn't want to be the damp squib.'

'You're far from being that,' Raz intoned, his dark deep drawl scraping down her taut spine in the tomblike silence of the basement in which only echoes and the soft background sound of moving water featured. 'I only wanted you to enjoy yourself this weekend. The tutoring you've received is not exactly fun—'

'Oh, I *have* enjoyed this break,' she hastened to assure him, because he had gone to a lot of trouble to organise the kind of stuff she had never known before, like travel and seeing historic sights and being spoiled.

She didn't want him to think that she was ungrateful for all those new experiences.

Zia clashed involuntarily with shimmering green eyes and her heartbeat landed somewhere in her throat and she felt her nipples tighten into painful points. The drops falling from the mini waterfall beside her seemed preternaturally loud and her tongue flicked out to nervously slick along her lower lip as she took an instinctive step back. His gaze narrowed and a pulsating buzz kicked up low in her belly, making her feel uncomfortably warm.

'Zia…' Raz muttered thickly.

'I guess we shouldn't be here alone together. I mean, Allie was warning me how careful I now need to be around men,' Zia muttered in embarrassment. 'She made it sound like Victorian times back in Mandovia…a clean reputation is everything.'

'She probably aimed that warning at you while thinking of me,' Raz remarked, shifting a step closer, hugely aroused as she continued to worry at her sultry pink lower lip and he only got harder and more heated. 'She views me as a predator with women.'

'Are you one?' Zia asked baldly.

'If you're looking for anything more than a flirtation, probably,' Raz conceded grudgingly.

'Oh, I'm not,' Zia admitted instantly. 'I don't want to be tied down to anyone.'

Taken aback by that bold admission, Raz rested a hand down on her slight shoulder, her damp skin silky soft to his touch. 'Neither do I.'

'Why is that?'

'Watched my parents fight through a dying marriage. It left an indelible impression,' he admitted.

Shivering below the clasp of his hand, Zia gazed up at him. 'I don't have that excuse. I don't have bad memories of my parents' marriage. I don't have *any* kind of memories. I suspect my mother couldn't possibly have been happy with a man like him but she was loyal and probably made the best of it,' she surmised.

Raz stared down into violet-blue eyes that shone like stars and it was as if there were a sudden hiccup in his brain. All of a sudden, he couldn't think, couldn't rationalise, couldn't recall all the many reasons why he should never ever touch her. The urge to connect with her was too powerful to resist. Without warning, he was reaching down to grip her other shoulder before sliding his hands down to hoist her up against him because, really, she was too small to kiss any other way. Lifting her to his level was non-negotiable.

'Shouldn't be doing this,' he groaned in an inadvertent, clumsy confession that infuriated him.

'Agreed, this is such a mistake,' Zia mumbled, all but drowning in the velvety soft touch of his shapely mouth on hers as he curved her spread thighs around his waist.

And it was electrifying, as if a literal lightning bolt struck her, a surge of heat engulfing her like a tropical storm. He was touching her *everywhere*. Her heart pounded in the moment that he crushed her against his heated muscular torso and kissed her breathless, his tongue delving and exploring, setting up a chain of physical reactions that were shockingly new to her.

So that was what real passion *should* feel like, she was thinking, dimly recalling those teenage explorations that had only disappointed and disillusioned, failing every time to reach her fond and hopeful expectations. Raz was dispensing the kind of seductive, provocative magic that tugged at every fibre of her quivering body, making her want more…and then *more.*

CHAPTER FOUR

ORAZIO GROUND ZIA down on his throbbing erection and inwardly cursed himself for the action. He was literally struggling to get a grip on himself, barely able to comprehend how he was behaving in a public place. His hands were cupping her superb breasts, thumbs stroking the engorged points through the fine fabric shielding her from him and nothing, absolutely nothing that he had ever experienced, had excited him to such an extent. He was shocked at his reaction to her and he didn't need the sound of a door opening at the top of the stairs to remind him that they were not enjoying perfect privacy.

'Are you all right, sir?' one of his security team called down.

'Thanks. I'm fine. I'll be finished soon,' he intoned as levelly as he could manage. It helped to lift Zia off his spread thighs and rise from the marble seat he had come down on and settle her carefully back into the softly lapping water.

'If you say sorry, I'll slap you!' Zia warned him, bristling like a cat suddenly plunged into an unwelcome bath, violet eyes huge in her flushed face as she stood up straight and turned away. 'We had a moment, that's all. No need for a post-mortem. We're both adults.'

Orazio didn't feel remotely like an adult in that instant. He felt like an overexcited teenager, which was very much *her* effect on him and a shatteringly original experience for him. There was nothing controlled or cautious or practical or sensible about those sensations. Those urges had simply overpowered him. *We had a moment.* He was tempted to say something in disagreement but resisted the urge, aware that she was ready to let her quick temper blow. He would've once said that she was much more volatile than him but, considering his own behaviour, he didn't believe that that was a fair assumption any longer. As she had reminded him, they were both adults and nothing more needed to be said.

He watched her disappear round the corner, leaking angry attitude from the set of her slight shoulders to the swagger of her truly phenomenal derrière. She had turned him inside out and upside down and she wasn't even aware of the fact. He dropped down into the water to kill his lingering arousal and then grabbed a towel to mount the stairs.

'I was alone down there,' he told his security team. 'You saw no one else.'

'Of course we didn't, sir.'

Zia went straight to her room and took an unnecessary shower in the vague hope that that would silence the pulsating hum at the centre of her body. That hum she had waited to feel with other men and had failed to find, that hum that signified a true physical connection. Wasn't it just her luck that Orazio should have provided that elusive spur of sexual awakening? That reality infuriated her. Orazio, who didn't want a relationship or anything else with her! Orazio, who was gloriously single and still enjoying his freedom? Nothing was likely to alter Orazio's priorities or his outlook overnight and change him into a potential partner.

She slid into her very comfortable bed and gazed up at the canopy overhead. She was alone with these new urges, alone as she had always been and she had to bury those reactions, forget she had ever felt them and with whom. Orazio was the wrong focus. She needed him as a friend, her sole ally in a strange, unfamiliar world, and the last thing she wanted to do was turn him into an enemy who might seek to avoid her.

No, she would remain impervious to his obvious attractions and indifferent to his charm because she wasn't a silly girl and had never had the freedom to be anything but sensible. Dwelling on what his mouth and his hands had felt like on her body would be downright foolish and she refused to go down that path with a male who had already made his position clear. No, she wasn't the type to long for a guy from afar, comparing every other male to his detriment. She was strong, practical and she would bounce into breakfast the next morning like a woman without a single care in the world.

A cautious note sounded in the depths of her brain as she recalled that she still had to tell Orazio about that theft accusation in London. She groaned out loud and squirmed at that challenge that still lay ahead. She wished she had Sausage to cuddle for comfort and missed him with a deep, pained ache because Sausage mightn't be the brightest little animal, but he was endlessly cuddly and affectionate. For a long time, that tiny dog had been her closest friend.

Alina had never been someone she could confide in. Their worst problems had been too much of a challenge for Alina and, increasingly aware of her nursemaid's growing mental and physical frailty, Zia had protected the older woman as best she could.

Orazio tensed as Zia walked out onto the terrace for breakfast, paused to admire the fabulous view of the mountains and then turned with her natural smile to greet everyone at the table. She looked like a teenager in a flowing cotton sundress the same colour as the blue sky above them, her black hair drawn up in a ponytail, her tiny feet shod in trainers.

'Do you have a swimsuit on underneath?' Allie asked her helpfully.

'Yes. I have an entire collection of them now,' Zia remarked with quiet pride.

Something clenched in Orazio's chest at the renewed awareness that she had gone without for so long. Ignored and forgotten about by both governments but fished back out of obscurity to play the role they now needed her to fulfil in the reunification. He wondered what she would choose to do, where she would go, when her six months in Mandovia were up. Would she stay on? Pursue her studies in her birth country or return to London?

'She'll get married, nothing surer,' Fiero forecast at his elbow in an undertone as though Orazio had shared his thoughts out loud. 'Six months spent meeting every eligible family heir and top businessman in Mandovia at all the fancy soirées ahead of her? She's beautiful and she'll be very much in demand. A huge number of men would like to bring a princess into the family.'

'For all you know she might be looking for another princess to keep her company, not a man!' Allie interposed in a sarcastic aside to her fiancé as Zia was ushered into a seat at the head of the table, facing Orazio.

Orazio shrugged both shoulders, deflecting further comment on Zia's prospects but hugely unsettled by his best friend's forecast. She would be a hell of a catch for the right guy, he acknowledged belatedly. Beautiful, brainy, able to speak several languages. Such a woman would bring gloss and opportunity to any family keen to raise their social status and there was a huge number of pretentious people in the upper echelons of both countries.

'So, what's on the itinerary today?' Zia asked cheerfully as she shredded a croissant and proceeded to heap blueberry jam onto every piece.

Their little moment in the spa pool *had* left her untouched, Orazio conceded in surprise. But what did he really know about her? The shy brush of her lips meeting his might have seemed relatively unpractised but what did he know about her past? Not that he was interested or cared or was even judgemental, he assured himself swiftly. He had sufficient experience of his own not to be negative about others who decided to enjoy the freedom of being an adult while they were able to do so.

Fiero chattered like a tour guide and Orazio noticed then that Zia's violet-blue gaze slanted past him at every opportunity. A tinge of satisfaction touched him then. He was being blanked and he knew that he deserved to be after what he had done. He owed her an apology for pretty much grabbing her, for taking advantage of their isolation and then taking off afterwards as though the hounds of hell were on his heels.

As their party left the hotel, he reached for her hand and squeezed it, looking down at her with brilliant green eyes. 'I'm sorry about last night. I was in the wrong—'

And then there was a yell and their security team was taking off in pursuit of a man who had apparently been concealed in the bushes by the hotel entrance.

'Well, there goes the neighbourhood,' Fiero groaned, hurrying them all into the sanctuary of the car. 'He got a photo of you holding her hand too! That's going to make the two of you look very friendly—'

'I thought we'd be safe here,' Orazio lamented, abruptly releasing her fingers as if they had burnt him.

'You're not safe anywhere, particularly with all the rumours currently doing the rounds about the lost Princess coming home to Mandovia,' Allie chipped in wryly. 'Why on earth were you holding her hand?'

'I stumbled. He was trying to steady me,' Zia fibbed, but with hot pink cheeks that would've fooled no one.

'Perhaps we won't be identified,' Orazio suggested.

'You're one of the most eligible bachelors in Europe. Of course, you'll be recognised!' Fiero told him impatiently.

Good-natured wrangling on that point filled the car, Allie claiming that a baseball hat and an unshaven jaw did little to conceal Orazio's famous features. Her own face still burning, Zia concentrated instead on looking out at the passing countryside and she was the first out of the car when they arrived at Hierapolis, the last of the ancient city ruins on their trip.

Again, a knowledgeable guide met them. Allie turned her ankle on a rough path and Fiero took her off to sit down in the shade. Alone with Orazio, Zia stiffened until she registered the parties of other tourists around them. It was not the place to make a confession about being accused of a theft. In a silence broken only by the guide's scholarly speeches, they appreciated the magnificent sight of the ancient theatre with its frontage that stretched to over a hundred yards in length.

The sun was relentless. Perspiration beaded her brow. Once they had seen the main sights Orazio asked the guide to take them to the Cleopatra pools to join their friends. They entered the thermal spring complex alone. There they found Allie reclining across a fallen Roman column in a pool with all the panache of a sea siren.

'You should come in. The water's lovely,' she called. 'Very warm and mineral-rich. It's easing my ankle.'

Sitting down nearby, Zia unbuttoned her dress and removed her trainers, rising in her plain blue swimsuit to step down into the inviting water and settle close to Allie to enjoy the refreshing embrace of water on her hot skin. Orazio had already fallen into a spirited conversation with Fiero and she saw cold drinks being brought to the men as they sat down below the palm trees. The whole time she was in the water, she remained insanely conscious of Orazio's scrutiny, and the weight of those piercing green eyes on her half-naked body infuriated her.

'Raz can't take his eyes off you,' Allie murmured half under her breath. 'I've never seen him being so obvious.'

'It's meaningless,' Zia responded breezily.

'I'll tell him off for you. I'm getting out. I'm dying for a drink.'

Zia cooled off in the deeper part of the pool and followed suit, emerging from a changing cubicle in record time to join the others in the shade where she gulped down water before they moved on. They did a tour of the stunning white travertine terraces of the Pamukkale pools but Zia merely bathed her toes alongside Allie, who was awkwardly using Fiero's arm to balance on. By mutual agreement they called it a day there and returned with relief to the air-conditioned cool of the car to head for lunch.

Lunch was served in a pretty village taverna and it was a fairly basic affair of fresh bread, salad and cheese. Orazio watched her every movement like a hawk. She was utterly unselfconscious and paid him absolutely no heed while she ate and drank and exchanged light conversation with his friends. She was remarkably self-contained for a woman of not quite twenty-three, he conceded. It was as though he had suddenly become invisible and he was not accustomed to that experience, no, not from *any* woman he had graced with his interest.

Yet here he was, reliving the knowledge that her pale skin was smooth as porcelain and had felt like soft satin beneath the sweep of his fingers. He didn't want to remember that, but he remembered it all too well. He was unlikely to soon forget the little soft moan she had loosed low in her throat when he had kissed her. Had there ever been a single sound *that* sexy? Even less quickly would he forget the full, firm weight of her beautiful breasts when he had merely brushed his palms over them. *Dio mio*, he was fantasising like a teenager about a kiss! And as hard as a rock at the recollection, throbbing heat pressing against his zip.

'We should get back on the road,' Orazio announced impatiently, rising to his full imposing height and crumpling his napkin to toss it on the table. 'We have a long drive back.'

Buried in a book on her e-reader, Zia lent little to the desultory chat during the drive. She still hadn't told Orazio about the theft thing and it was worrying at her like a nagging tooth. The right moment hadn't arisen, she reasoned, so she would have to pounce on the first moment she knew he was alone on the yacht. After all, she was fairly sure that he would be returning to Mandovia the next day and nobody had told her yet when she would be leaving or when she would be deemed presentable enough to be shown off to the Mandovian people.

Their return to the *Sea Empress* was enlivened by the clutch of paparazzi shouting questions and flashing cameras as they boarded the motor launch. Zia realised that nobody had yet identified her, which felt like a relief, but she knew that it was only a matter of time before that would change. At present she was simply assumed to be Orazio's latest female companion and caught up in the surge of publicity that always surrounded the young King's social outings.

Alina was waiting for her on the yacht, full of chatter about the yacht staff and of how during Zia's absence she had toured every inch of the giant boat while being treated like a queen. Zia showered and changed for dinner and then asked the nearest stewardess where Orazio was. Learning that he was in his cabin, she lifted her chin and asked where it was.

Allie dressed for dinner and so Zia had as well in a long, light, flowy skirt and a camisole top in shades of toning purple. Everything she wore was designer, everything beautifully fashioned and tailored to her exact size, a luxury that must've come at an eye-watering cost for the government. That they had provided her with such an expensive wardrobe for her debut in Mandovia underlined the reality that they believed she could be important in her birth country, even if it would only be as a useful figurehead in the much-anticipated reunification.

She knocked on the cabin door and waited. A voice barked out something within. She knocked again and waited, biting apprehensively at her lower lip.

Finally, the door opened, framing an impatient Orazio, only a towel wrapped round his lean hips, water still dripping down his bronzed bare chest. Glittering green eyes assailed hers, surprise tautening his lean, darkly handsome features. 'How can I help you?' he said tautly.

'I'm sorry to have disturbed you but I have something important to tell you and it's not something I would want to share with other people present,' she admitted tightly.

Raz thrust the door wider. 'You'd better come in. I'll get some clothes on.'

Zia was flushed at what felt like an intrusion on her part, but she was tempted to tell him not to bother getting dressed on her account. After all, stripped, he bore an even closer resemblance to a Greek god of myth and legend. Every inch of him was lean, honed, muscular and golden perfection. A damp awareness shimmied through her every nerve ending, making her feel hot, bothered and embarrassed. Only with difficulty did she muster her thoughts again to focus on the reason she had sought him out alone. He strode out of what must've been a dressing room, sheathed in tight faded jeans and a linen shirt, still hanging open to expose his mouth-watering chest.

Breathing in deep, Zia burst straight into speech. 'I have something rather shocking to tell you and, obviously, I didn't want an audience for it,' she admitted starkly. 'But I *have* to tell you about it in case it causes trouble in the future.'

Dark brows pleating in bewilderment, Orazio stared down at her. 'Shocking? Is this something in your past?'

'My very recent past in London,' she explained uneasily. 'I was accused of theft at the hotel where I worked by a Mandovian citizen—'

Orazio's lean, strong face clenched hard and he swore only half under his breath. *'Theft?'* he stressed in disbelief.

'I didn't do it. I was falsely accused!' Zia slammed back at him defensively.

'Isn't that what every thief says when they're caught?' Orazio countered unhelpfully, his taut patrician features unyielding and judgemental.

Zia flung up her head. 'I don't like your attitude!' she fired back truthfully.

'I don't like the sound of what you're telling me,' Raz riposted truthfully, because any accusation of previous dishonesty would wreck Zia's reputation before she even reached the public stage.

Angry tears lashed the backs of Zia's wide eyes because she had somehow expected a more sympathetic response from him and now she wondered why. After all, Raz was the Mandovian monarch, a representative of the throne and the supposed repository of Mandovian moral values and everyone knew that there wasn't much *give* in those values when it came to public figures.

'Sit down,' Raz instructed less abrasively. 'Take a deep breath and tell me the whole story.'

She looked so beautiful in that instant that even if there had been a gun aimed at him, he couldn't have told her to calm down, watch her tone and wise up in her delivery because what she had just confessed was a very grave matter.

Unfortunately for him, she was already drawing in great gasps of air to sustain herself, her narrow chest heaving, her barely contained breasts shimmying like some sensual mirage below the fine fabric covering them. Purple was definitely her colour yet he had believed it was blue when he first saw her in the sundress. But the purple shades she wore highlighted her striking violet-blue eyes. Much too beautiful to be alone with him in his cabin. For a split second he thought of propping the cabin door open and then he asked himself if they were all living in Victorian England and shook off the idea while such an incendiary subject was under discussion. He could not risk such a dialogue being overheard.

There was nowhere to sit but the wide divan bed and Zia planted herself on the edge of it, her skirt pooling on the polished wooden floor. 'If it's any consolation…er, as far as I know the theft thing isn't still hanging over me. Massimo Caccia got me out of trouble. It was like magic. One minute it was all hovering over my head…

and the next minute it was gone. He swore it would be buried and forgotten and at the time I was so grateful I didn't question that statement.'

'Massimo... Massimo Caccia? He *knows* about this? *He* got you out of this mess?' Orazio fired at her with incredulous bite. 'How can he have been there with you when it happened?'

'I have no idea...but he *did* help me.'

In miserable silence, Zia suppressed a sigh, wondering at the flash of furious disbelief that had tightened his lean, strong face. Why shouldn't Massimo have been there when he had purported to be working at the embassy at the time?

Raz paced away a few steps. If she had believed her cabin was big, his was far bigger and positively grand. He swung back to her, caramel-blond hair flopping untidily over his brow that he brushed back with an impatient hand. 'Tell me *everything*,' he urged intently. 'Leave nothing out, no matter how trivial it might seem now.'

And she told him the whole story then, including the identity of the rich hotel guest, at whose name he literally winced, before she concluded with Massimo's arrival in the proceedings when he had taken over the hotel manager's office.

'Massimo Caccia has nothing to do with the embassy in London,' Raz told her with a frown as he continued to pace. 'I don't know why you would assume he could work there or why he would let you believe that.'

Zia outlined the proposal that Massimo had made to her in which he had promised to make the theft charge go away. 'You see, I didn't have a choice about whether or not I came to Mandovia,' she admitted shamefacedly then, certain that that truth would make him think less of her character. 'That theft charge would've ruined my life.'

'Of course, it would've done,' Raz gritted, his shrewd brain working on the facts she had given him and his own knowledge of the situation. Caccia and the government had wanted the lost Princess of Upper Mandovia to return to represent the former republic as an important reminder of their heritage and to, hopefully, unite her people. Had they wanted her at any cost? Caccia certainly had. But the government would never have given him permission to entrap her in such a manner. Very probably, Caccia had pulled off her miraculous return entirely on his own by plotting and planning to put her within his power.

Scorching anger gripped Orazio, who rarely got that angry about anything. Even so, the conviction that Massimo Caccia had treated Zia unpardonably, and put her through hurt and humiliation simply to suit his own ends and show what a slick operator he could be at her expense, remained uppermost. 'I suspect that you were manipulated and blackmailed! It's too neat to have been anything other than a set-up to ensnare you. No way was Massimo hanging about on the spot to step in and save you by sheer good luck!' he asserted with pure rage biting through his dark, deep drawl. 'I'm very relieved that you told me. Don't worry about it any more. *I* will deal with this.'

Zia was shocked by his change of attitude. 'So, you *don't* think that I'm a thief, then?' she pressed hesitantly, that being the only element that seemed truly important to her.

Raz paused in his pacing to turn back to her. 'Obviously not, *piccola mia.* I believe that Massimo wanted you back in Mandovia no matter what it cost and he acted accordingly to make that possible.'

Release from the terrible fearful tension that had been holding Zia rigid sliced through her and an inevitable weakness followed, loosening all her taut muscles. Her shoulders dropped and the flood of relieved tears that followed was unstoppable, streaming down her face as she stifled a choked sob of reaction. It had seemed for a few terrifying moments that Orazio believed that she *was* a thief and that fear had horrified her, which she supposed only proved how naïve she could still be. After all, why would he have faith in her honesty when he barely knew her? Why would he trust her word? Assume her to be innocent just because she said she was?

Orazia studied her shaking shoulders in consternation. He didn't know what to do with a crying woman. He had grown up with a mother who regularly threw hysterical scenes when she was upset and his intervention had only ever made matters worse. A sympathetic audience only stoked his mother to greater heights of bitterness and resentment. He had learned to walk away and allow her to get it out of her system. He could scarcely have emulated his grandfather, who had once slapped his daughter's face in an effort to calm her down. In any case that intervention hadn't worked either and the older man had had to grovel for months afterwards to win his daughter's forgiveness.

But strangely enough, leaving Zia to cry alone struck

him as unforgivably cruel and something stronger than he was seemed to propel him across the room to offer her comfort. He sank down on the bed beside her and closed a supportive arm round her tiny frame. 'It's all right. It's over now. Don't worry about it,' he muttered uncertainly while questioning what he was doing when he had already decided to keep his distance from Zia.

Zia drew strength from his support and unexpected warmth. 'I can't help worrying about it. What happens if I'm introduced to this Sofia Marone and she recognises me?'

'Massimo's far too wily not to have taken care of that potential problem,' Orazio opined.

'I'm not sure that she would even recognise me. She had no reason to know I was from Mandovia and I never spoke to her in Italian. My hair was covered as well because the hotel thinks it's more hygienic and I didn't have any make-up on either—'

'By the sound of it, I think it's highly unlikely that she would recognise you. Put it behind you now and I will look into the matter for you…discreetly,' he told her gently, squeezing her slim shoulders, and he was momentarily stunned by the comfort he was carefully administering. But then he had upset her and he should have been more tactful to begin with, he reasoned self-critically. The more he understood about the life she had led to date, the more spoiled he felt himself to have been. The only adversity he had ever faced had been in tough business deals and neither his reputation nor his wealth had ever depended on them. He no longer marvelled at the maturity beyond her years that Zia demonstrated or her self-control and feistiness. She had learned the hard way that she needed to put on a tough front to protect herself.

'Thanks...you've been much kinder than I expected,' Zia told him truthfully, and as she stood up she dabbed a light kiss on his cheek, only to find both of his arms closing round her and dragging her back to him again.

'Oh, I think that we can do better than that, *piccola mia*,' Orazio quipped, drinking in the scent of coconut and orange blossom that emanated from her hair and her skin. She smelled like a very tempting and stimulating fruit bowl on a hot day.

'But we *shouldn't*,' Zia reminded him cautiously.

'We won't do anything to frighten the horses,' he teased wickedly, tilting her back down to him with easy strength.

Glittering green eyes collided with hers and stopped her breath in its tracks. Goose bumps broke out on her arms and her breathing hitched as she tried to fill her lungs again. The hunger he couldn't hide showed in that smouldering appraisal and ignited her own. Wild anticipation filled her and lit a tiny flickering flame low in her belly.

He brushed his lips across hers in an exploratory move and she tipped her head back and parted her lips with a responsiveness that punched him in the stomach with its simplicity. And that fast, Orazio, who prided himself on his self-discipline and intelligence, forgot every reason he shouldn't be touching her and succumbed. He kissed her breathless, pulling her down on top of him, one hand with splayed fingers diving into the silky depths of her hair to hold her fast while he hungrily plundered her sweet mouth over and over again.

Zia's head swam almost giddily as he brought her back down on the bed. She could taste his hunger and it matched hers, which was a revelation. She wanted to flatten him to the bed and take thorough advantage of him and she had never felt that aroused around a man before. Nobody had ever kissed her with such driving passion and she wanted more. He pinned her under him on the mattress, one big hand moulding the thrust of an unbound breast while long fingers tugged on a straining, sensitive nipple.

A little cry was wrenched from low in her throat as he bent his mouth there instead to capture the pointed peak through the fine fabric screening it from him and suck on it. Her back arched, her hips rising in invitation at that intimacy.

'How the hell,' he asked, half laughing in his frustration, having found neither zip nor buttons to unfasten, 'do I get you out of this contraption?'

And that understandable question was like a shower of ice on her overheated skin, chilling her to the bone with consternation. 'You *don't*,' she responded stiffly, having stilled, then shifting in an abrupt move to snake out from under him and roll athletically off the bed to check her reflection in the nearest mirror, fingers smoothing her hair and twitching straight her skirt, rubbing away the smudging of her lipstick inflicted by that bout of enthusiastic kissing.

Bracing himself on his strong arms, Orazio sprang off the bed, seething with arousal, seething with her for taking flight. 'Zia—'

She whirled round, huge violet-blue eyes troubled

and stormy. 'No, don't say anything. You know we can't do this. We have to be friends and only that—'

'Friends with benefits?' Orazio sliced in, more than a little desperate and embarrassed by the fact because he did not think a woman had ever lit him up so fast and then left him close to begging. But somehow, Zia did, and she did it without even trying.

'I think that would be too hard to navigate without people finding out,' she parried, a hint of steel in her cooling gaze now. 'And if we got found out, you'd be expected to marry me and I would be labelled the temptress, so neither of us want those consequences—'

'Obviously not, but an attraction this explosive is a challenge to contain,' Orazio argued.

'Better we stop now than get carried away—'

'Have you *ever* got carried away with a man?' Orazio fenced helplessly.

'No,' Zia conceded thoughtfully. 'But if it's any consolation, I *could* do with you. Only right now my life has taken a positive turn at last and I don't plan to mess it up by making any mistakes. You would be a *huge* mistake. If I stay on in Mandovia, I have no desire at all to be seen as one of your rejected lovers. To be frank, I have too much pride to occupy that group.'

Orazio swallowed hard. He had never been told no with such calm, logical reasoning. In reality, no was not a word he had ever heard in the bedroom. By the time he got a woman to the bed, it was a done deal and everyone knew what was going to happen next. Only Zia was different, entirely different in every way.

'Last night was your fault but tonight was mine. I shouldn't have come here to be alone with you even though I knew I had to speak to you alone. Let's stick to offices or public places from now on,' Zia suggested ruefully. 'I don't think we can be trusted alone in private.'

It shook Orazio to have that spelt out. He didn't think he had ever met a woman less afraid to spell out a harsh truth. They were both responsible for a lack of restraint and she had no problem owning her part in it. Raised by parents who had never been willing to acknowledge fault in a single one of their worst missteps, Orazio was impressed much more than he wanted to be.

Aching with suppressed lust, once she had left his cabin he stripped for a cold shower and broke out in a literal cold sweat at the prospect of taking Zia back to Mandovia the next day. Distance, distance, he reminded himself fiercely, don't even think about her.

CHAPTER FIVE

'THE PHOTOS OF you two as a couple are all over social media,' Allie informed Raz and Zia as she scrolled through her phone at speed during the flight in a private jet. 'The paps will swamp you at the airport!'

'We weren't doing anything suspect,' Zia protested, refusing to look Orazio in the eye, something she had contrived to do quite successfully since the night before when she had joined everyone for dinner. Having first changed into a different outfit, of course, one without a damp patch on the bodice that might awaken unwise memories and responses.

'I don't think Raz has been seen in public holding a girl's hand since he was forced to play Joseph to my terrified Mary in primary school,' Allie confided unhelpfully. 'Usually he's very hands-off...'

They had left the yacht not long after dawn with all her many suitcases of new clothes. Alina, quite overpowered by the threat of spending even *one* night in a royal castle, had already asked if it would be all right for her to be picked up by her nephew at the airport so that she could return to Upper Mandovia and visit her widowed sister and her family in their mountain village.

Zia envied Alina her smooth escape from the new world awaiting her, yet did not begrudge her former nursemaid a reunion with the family she hadn't seen in almost twenty years. But nerves were even now eating Zia alive. Orazio had already fielded several phone calls from government ministers relating to plans and changed itineraries. In short, her introduction to Mandovia was being moved up to meet popular demand. But what was even worse was that, seemingly, Orazio's plans were being changed as well. He was now scheduled to accompany her to Upper Mandovia, to present what the prime minister had described as a 'united front' for the benefit of both countries. And Orazio had gritted his teeth and tried to reason his way out of that new plan, only he had got nowhere.

Zia would not have dared to admit that, although she was avoiding him in most ways like the plague, the knowledge that he would be around as backup loosened the tight knot of anxiety deep in her stomach. She wasn't yet ready to go it alone and she knew it. She also knew that he would prevent her from making any terrible errors, that he knew everything there was to know about stupid protocol and that no PR person at her elbow could ever replace him. She was so grateful that he would be accompanying her that she would even pretend that she had not heard him declare in sheer exasperation on the phone that he was '*not* a babysitter'! Much could be forgiven of a man who was finding his immediate future inconveniently and unfairly twinned and rearranged along with hers.

He wanted a break from her and why shouldn't he? It wasn't as though they were related in any way or as if she were *his* responsibility. A responsibility he definitely didn't want would have been a more accurate statement. After all, he had done his bit, organising the tutors, allowing her to stay on his yacht, making her feel welcome while remaining honest with her. What more could be expected of him?

Allie had advised her on what to wear to disembark, a rather plain dress and matching short-sleeved jacket in green. Orazio insisted she step out first ahead of him. As a barrage of flashing cameras greeted her she froze and tried to retreat, but Orazio welded a hand to her spine to prevent that and pushed her forward so that he could stand beside her. 'Might as well give them the money shot they're looking for with the two of us together,' he said drily.

A flush lit her cheeks as they crossed the tarmac to greet the hovering line of officials awaiting them, Orazio now noticeably separate from her. She straightened her slender spine, lifted her chin and moved forward, determined to accomplish what she had trained to do. And then the polite handshakes, greetings and the shock of being addressed as 'Your Highness' were done and she was tucked into a limousine fronted by outriders on motorbikes and accompanied by a posse of black security vehicles.

'How on earth do you manage to live like this?' she whispered, shell-shocked by the fuss, to Orazio.

'I usually drive myself away from the airport. I have security, of course,' he advanced wryly. 'No, it's *your* arrival that is creating all the pomp and ceremony today. Your first steps back onto Mandovian soil—'

'Good heavens,' she mumbled shakily.

'In Upper Mandovia you will be treated to adoring crowds. Here you're more of an unknown quantity but everyone's curious to see us together.'

'That's silly,' she deflected in more discomfort than ever at that admission.

'*We* know that but unfortunately the public would prefer us to be fairy-tale characters rather than more ordinary people.'

'Well, there's nothing fairy tale about me,' Zia quipped as the limo swept through tall imposing gates and her mouth ran dry at the sight of the building on the rising slope ahead of them: the royal castle, built of dark stone and dating back to medieval times. It was huge and rather gothic with many large towers and turrets, ironically very much like a property straight out of a child's storybook.

'Isn't there? Lost princess down on her luck forced to clean for a living? Rescued… I say rescued *questionably…*from the Wicked Witch?' Orazio teased with sudden amusement. 'Of course the public is hungry for every piece of information they can find out about you. Now you only need a handsome prince to complete the charmed circle.'

'Are there any around?' Zia laughed.

'Not in Mandovia that I know of.'

'That's good,' Zia said. 'I'm not in the mood for a handsome prince and I've always felt that women should try to rescue themselves from difficult situations…although, bearing in mind my own experiences, that's not always possible.'

'One of my legal team is waiting to speak to you

about your inheritance of the London house. He has questions for you to answer.'

'That should be interesting,' Zia muttered, still wondering if it could be true that all along that handsome house had belonged to her while she had scrabbled for an existence in the damp basement and scrubbed Sandrine's floors.

A clutch of staff was already waiting at the castle doors. Zia stepped out and Orazio performed introductions and, as they moved indoors, a sharp little bark alerted her to Sausage's arrival.

The miniature dachshund hurtled towards her like a guided missile and she got down on the tiled floor as the little dog frantically bounced round her, ears flying, tongue licking, little paws grasping and dancing. A deep-based mournful howl sounded and Sausage broke off his welcome to growl a threat in response.

Zia lifted her dog up in her arms and stood, telling him off when she saw a pair of massive sleek mastiffs standing still only a few feet away.

'Sit!' Raz instructed and the two dogs instantly sat. 'These are my dogs, Bear and Wolf.'

'They're very well trained,' Zia said enviously. 'Sausage can't sit without wriggling frantically and he's terribly bossy around other dogs.'

Orazio watched her introduce herself to his pets while the ubiquitous Sausage attempted with pedalling legs to escape his mistress's grip. 'Give him to me,' he urged.

Zia handed the little animal over and he went limp in Orazio's grasp as though he had been sedated and licked at his hand as if in apology. 'Gosh, you little sneak!'

she complained at her pet's sudden attack of good behaviour as she knelt down to get acquainted with Bear and Wolf, who, released from command, gazed calmly up at her as she petted them.

'How did you acquire Sausage?'

'One of Sandrine's boyfriends gave him to her one Christmas, not knowing that she hates animals. They broke up but she expected him to come back to her and so she kept the dog. Then when Alina and I moved down to the basement flat, Sausage came with us and never left again.'

Handing back Sausage, he passed her over to the hovering housekeeper and mentioned that he would see her at the official reception that evening.

Zia was relieved to see that while the castle looked medieval, it was fairly contemporary inside the walls. But there was a mountain of twisting stone steps to be climbed up to her room, all the same, and she reckoned they would keep her fit, although she didn't expect to stay in the castle more than her one agreed night.

Her room—well, she would have called it a suite—was in the South Tower with a panoramic view of the gardens beneath. The appointments were amazing. She was shown a custom-designed dressing room, where maids were already unpacking her cases, a dream of a circular bathroom and, finally, her big bedroom with its canopied, thoroughly decadent bed festooned in blue and silver drapery. A reading nook complete with opulent couch and crowded bookshelves occupied one corner like an invitation.

'This was the former Queen's accommodation,' the

housekeeper told her brightly. 'She spent a lot of time up here.'

Orazio's mother, who had dropped her title along with her royal husband and moved back to Venezuela.

'It's lovely,' Zia remarked appreciatively, surprised that Orazio hadn't had her stashed in a more ordinary guestroom.

'It needed refreshing. It hasn't been used since Queen Luisa departed. By the way, the solicitor, Mr Accardi, and his assistant are waiting to see you in the room next door.'

Zia walked straight into that meeting without hesitation. She was keen to learn the facts of her situation. No, she had never seen a lawyer about her inheritance or received any official notice or papers or letters when she reached eighteen years of age. No, she had not signed over anything to Sandrine Beccari. She was then shown a couple of documents and the signatures purporting to be hers.

'That's not even a very good copy of my signature,' she said with a frown.

Paper and a pen were advanced to her and she was asked to write her usual signature, which she did several times, her pin-neat writing style, taught by Alina, very different from the carelessly scrawled name on the documents.

She was asked if she was willing to go to court to have the matter cleared up. 'If necessary, yes. I've nothing to lose and everything to gain,' she pointed out. 'If Sandrine forged my signature—and, clearly, she did—she deserves to be punished for it.'

After that interview, Zia felt free to change into jeans

and a light top and take Sausage down to the gardens for what remained of the afternoon. There she wandered below the trees, enjoying the relative coolness after the searing heat of Türkiye, while Sausage romped about chasing and fetching a tennis ball Zia found lying in a flower bed.

Orazio watched her from his office window, his dogs by his side, whining to go down and join the fun with the miniature terrorist, who was apparently quite a bully in dog terms.

'I can't believe you put her in the Queen's Tower,' Fiero exclaimed.

'It's only for one night. And with the wardrobe she's got now, she needs a dressing area where a maid can do her hair for her.'

'Stay away from her this evening. The household is already talking up a storm at what they see as preferential treatment.'

'Well, then, they need to wise up. Treating Zia in any way as lesser than me would rouse fierce partisan sympathies in Upper Mandovia. The PM is now worried they'll back away from the reunification and put a crown on her head.'

'They're broke. They can't afford a crown or anything else.'

'Didn't think of that but it's a fair point.'

The talk devolved to politics while Orazio watched Zia playing artlessly with her dog. Silky black hair catching in the breeze, her slender shapely figure enhanced by the casual outfit. Images from the night before assailed him and arousal shot through him again like a burning torch, tightening the fit of his tailored trousers. He almost cursed out loud. He didn't believe that he had ever wanted a woman the way he wanted her. Was that because she was forbidden fruit?

That evening, Allie joined Zia in her bedroom when she was almost ready for the reception. 'Wow…' the blonde gasped. 'That is some dress!'

Zia had been advised on what to wear for an official reception. Her dress was a shimmering silver sheath that left her arms and shoulders bare but merely skimmed her curves and revealed nothing. Her hair was up in a fancy curled design and studded with pearl pins, since she didn't have any jewellery to wear.

'I wasn't expecting to see you again so soon,' Zia admitted.

'I had to call into the office to catch up on the way home. Home for me is here in the castle, by the way. I share Fiero's apartment. In addition, my company organised tonight's reception,' she advanced with quiet pride. 'They were in a hurry and we specialise at speed, so we were picked. It's a buffet and drinks because there are too many guests for anything else.'

'I wish I could say I'm looking forward to it, but I'm not,' Zia admitted with her trademark bluntness. 'Everyone's curiosity about me is intimidating.'

'You'll get used to it,' Allie forecast as she accompanied her downstairs, where Zia was greeted by Matteo, the suave young PR guy chosen to stay by her side throughout the event.

Her attention swerved straight to Orazio the minute she entered the room. She reasoned that that was natural when he was so much taller than the majority of people and his caramel-blond hair shone below the lights of the crowded room. He was surrounded by a clique of women glittering with jewellery and sporting high-fashion gowns.

'The centre of attention as always,' Allie giggled, leaning close. 'Sometimes I feel sorry for him. Some of those women are so desperate to catch his eye.'

'I imagine he's very much in demand.'

'Young, single, gorgeous, a king and a billionaire.' Allie counted off her fingers. 'He's got all the exciting attraction of an undiscovered goldmine.'

'And he *knows* it,' Zia chipped in very softly.

'Sadly, yes. Couldn't fail to. Girls were falling at his feet even when he was a teenager visiting for the summer.'

'You have to be our princess,' a voice interposed and a young dark-haired man with a ready smile stepped in front of her. 'And you look suitably regal.'

Zia laughed because there was something endearingly boyish about his twinkling eyes and dimples. 'I'm not at all regal.'

'May I introduce myself?' he asked, extending a hand for hers. 'I am Giancarlo Marone. Are you really called Annunziata or is there a catchier tag to be had?'

'Zia,' she provided, amused against her will as he carried her hand to his lips and kissed it like some old-fashioned smoothie.

'But addressing the Princess as Your Highness would be the correct approach,' Allie slotted in from the side.

'Your Highness,' Giancarlo quipped with the same dancing grin, dark eyes holding hers with a warmth that telegraphed just how attractive he found her. 'May I introduce you to my family?'

'There's an official receiving line in ten minutes,' Allie interposed.

'But I don't want to wait,' Giancarlo mocked.

'I'm afraid you'll have to.' Zia retrieved her hand calmly. 'The reception has a very strict time schedule.'

'Biggest womaniser in Mandovia but he's from your part of the country,' Allie hissed in her ear warningly as she carried her deeper into the room. 'Son of our richest resident and destined to be a count when his father goes.'

'Told you the sharks would be out in force,' Fiero quipped from the far side of the room, following Orazio's gaze to that same revealing encounter. 'Giancarlo is not letting the grass grow under his feet. If this were a race, he would already have won. Did you see her smile?'

Rage coiled like a black mamba in Orazio's chest and he wanted to hit something. How dared Giancarlo Marone approach Zia so boldly, all smiles, not to mention that smarmy kissing of her hand? His even white teeth gritted. He wondered why he was so annoyed. After all, Giancarlo would be a very suitable match for her. He should be wishing her well. Why wasn't he?

Giancarlo continued to hover in Zia's vicinity and was right there by her side when his parents appeared in the line—separately because Giancarlo's mother was now an ex-wife, and the new wife was the lady who had accused Zia of stealing her diamond brooch. She curtsied and greeted Zia without the smallest sign of recognition and Zia didn't even have time to panic before she was being guided on down the line of introductions.

Relief spread through her that that potential hazard had been faced down and was no longer a concern. Giancarlo squired her to the buffet. It was time to sit down and eat and he introduced her to his younger sister, Claudia, a vapid beauty, who could barely stay in her seat when Orazio was anywhere within hailing distance, so keen was she to attract his attention. Courtesy forced Orazio to come over and speak. He was clearly well acquainted with the siblings and Zia was insanely conscious of his gaze resting on her as she chattered to Giancarlo, whom she found entertaining, if indiscreet, company with his little gossipy insider stories about certain VIPs present.

She ate little and listened while Giancarlo ambitiously outlined his plan to take her on a picnic on horseback in Upper Mandovia. Since she had never been on a horse in her life, she was parting her lips to admit as much when Orazio intervened without warning. 'Zia is only now learning to ride horses. She won't be ready any time soon for a mountain trek.'

Zia seized the excuse gratefully and smiled. 'Yes, but when I am ready I will let you know.'

There was a smoulder in Orazio's lingering scrutiny that made her recall the exhilarating burn of his mouth on hers and she got a little short of breath, that buzz at the heart of her igniting without warning, leaving a dull, nagging ache in its wake. She felt uncomfortable and excused herself. In the cloakroom she ran her wrists under cold water and breathed in and breathed out slowly. Orazio had stayed away from her all evening and she had been prepared for that, hadn't she? She knew that he didn't want to link their names together and risk creating more rumours about their relationship.

So why did his distance now hurt and make her feel small and dismissed? Pondering that conundrum and annoyed with herself for even having such thoughts, she was startled when her hand was grasped and she was tugged into one of the rooms she was walking past. She only just swallowed a frightened shriek and exclaimed, *'What—?'*

Her dazed violet eyes focused in consternation on Orazio. She felt reassured then that she was safe and her bemused gaze skittered over their surroundings. Shelves packed with crockery and glasses lined the walls of what was obviously some sort of storage closet. 'What the heck—?'

'Giancarlo is a friend of mine,' Orazio volunteered. 'But he's also a notorious playboy.'

'Oh, is that all?' Zia retorted with wry amusement. 'I'm way past the age and experience to be seduced. I haven't spent the last almost twenty-three years living down a burrow, protected from all predatory men.'

'I only wanted to warn you,' Orazio said coldly.

Zia gazed up at him unimpressed, violet-blue eyes sharp with withering cynicism and inner knowledge with the hurt inside her crushed down hard. 'No, you're jealous,' she contradicted. 'You don't want me but you don't want anyone else to want me either.'

And that unlovely and very blunt truth engulfed Orazio like a bucket of cold water flung over his head. He *was* jealous, he, who had never been jealous over a woman in his life! He was appalled. He didn't get attached, didn't attach strings to any woman, held no expectations, practised a simple easy-come-easy-go outlook. Only not with Zia. The very idea of another guy putting his hands on Zia's tiny curvy body filled him with a fury that he could not adequately explain.

It was more than lust, more than possessiveness, more than anything he had felt for a woman before. And equally honestly, those innate feelings for her made his blood run cold because he didn't *want* to feel like that. He wanted the coolness he was accustomed to feeling with a woman, desire but nothing out of control, nothing excessive. And then Zia appeared and everything he experienced in relation to her was excessive, obsessive… inexcusable in his circumstances, where staying in control was an absolute rule he had never strayed from before. His cold, empty childhood had taught him to stay in control to protect himself. He had never known what it was to be loved during those crucial years of development. Yet now, for the first time ever, he was acting on urges that verged far from his usual rigid self-discipline and he found it unnerving. Even worse was the reality that *she* was calling *him* to account!

'Let me tell you the difference between you and Giancarlo,' Zia framed shakily, increasingly angry with him for his hypocritical behaviour. 'You're both… I assume…manwhores. Giancarlo only wants me because his father practically purrs when I appear and he would like his son to bring a princess home, so, no, I'm not going to fall for anything that obvious. You, though, want me for me, for my body and nothing else, but at least it's authentic—'

'Stop talking like that about yourself!' Orazio cut in,

furious with her for her outspokenness, for saying what he would not have dared to say and looking him levelly in the eye as she did it, truly fearless. 'It's vulgar—'

'No, it's not. It's honest and I always prefer to be honest. I want you and you want me but it's never going anywhere because of who you are. I understand. I even respect that but this, this dragging me into a blasted crockery cupboard, which could cause a dreadful scandal, is offensive,' she condemned. 'Either step away or step up to the plate!'

Orazio swore vehemently in Italian and she didn't even have the grace to look embarrassed. Her starlit eyes glimmered below the light and then the light went out, plunging the tiny space into darkness, and that was the only invitation he needed. He reached for her and lifted her up against him and crushed her ripe peach-tinted lips under his and nothing had ever felt so right or so necessary to him. He meshed his seeking fingers into her glorious hair, hating that the glossy strands were up and out of his reach because he loved her hair hanging loose and silky.

'Raz!' she gasped.

'I can't think of anyone but you!' he growled.

'Only cos I said no!'

'I'm not that basic.'

'Are you sure of that?' she mumbled, locking her arms round his shoulders to stay vertical, wincing at the crashing rattle of crockery knocking together as he braced her up against the shelves behind her. His velvety soft mouth pried her lips open and his tongue plunged and an ache and an agony of need shot through her like a river of hot lava.

He settled her down on the edge of what felt like a table...*was* a table, she registered dimly, blinking as the motion sensor light flickered on again, illuminating his intent lean, hard-boned face. He was skimming up the hem of her dress, long supple fingers caressing the skin of her inner thighs and she was trembling and on the merest knife edge, craving what she knew she shouldn't have, feeling that it would be *different* with him. The whole fantasy scenario, Zia, she sniped at herself with an inner snort of disbelief. But then he traced the heated centre of her, so sensitive beneath the thin strip of material now stretched taut between her spread thighs. All of a sudden she couldn't think at all and was wholly at the mercy of teasing sensation as he brushed aside the barrier and traced his fingers along her cleft, delicately dipping into her wet depths while his thumb circled the bud of her desire.

What followed was like nothing that she had ever felt before. Rocketing, shooting spears of pleasure and excitement gripped her and then, before she could even begin to collect herself, she was blinded by an intense climax that scorched through her and left her limp. She couldn't credit that her body had reacted so quickly, so easily, taking all that unresolved tension and yearning and then simply blowing it out of the sky and away. It had been amazing and she was in awe.

But when he dipped his head and kissed her again, a strangled sound escaped her, a sound of lingering want and need and everything she knew she despised, a *weak* sound. She tore her mouth free, wanting him so intensely but refusing to give way to that seething heat in her blood and the reawakened burn at her feminine core. 'Let me down,' she told him. 'I'm not doing this with you!'

'Are you a virgin?' he growled.

'For goodness' sake, no!' she snapped with mortified impatience as she questioned everything that had happened between them and cringed for her own total vulnerability. 'I was a normal teenager with the usual experiences. But you're absolutely wrong for me and you know it. At this stage of my life, I want a relationship, not some hole-in-the-corner fling. And if you can't offer me the real thing, then have the decency to let me go and don't interfere in the choices I may make.'

Slowly, carefully, Orazio lifted her to lower her back to the floor, his teeth gritting as she brushed against his rigid erection. 'Have the decency', yes, those words had hit him squarely where they hurt because he knew he was just chasing sex. Wasn't that all he had ever done? Only this time, the urge was different, he acknowledged. It was more like being driven by an irresistible, insane force that he couldn't stop and it both bemused and intimidated him. The light went off again and then back on as he stepped back from her.

At that point, the door opened without any warning whatsoever, making both of them flinch. Fiero peered in, sheer astonishment etched on his expressive face as he took in their messy appearance. 'Are you both crazy? The castle is crawling with VIPs and journalists tonight.'

'I'll go and freshen up,' Zia announced frigidly, knowing that Orazio had untidied her hair and smeared her make-up. She was still furious with him but also still furiously hot for the continuation of that kiss and his touch. The dichotomy of those opposing feelings made her feel shaky, uneasy and wildly confused, as if she no longer knew herself.

'So, when's the wedding?' Fiero asked the instant she was out of hearing.

'Are you serious?'

'No, I'm trying to work out what's going on here when I've never once seen you behave recklessly before. I'm starting to wonder if you're falling for her.'

Orazio smoothed down his tailored dinner jacket with a ridiculously unsteady hand because he was still reliving the instant she had melted into bliss and his own powerful satisfaction, even though his own needs had not been met in even the smallest way. Strangely, for the first time ever, that loaded word, 'marriage', didn't strike cold horror into his bones. He imagined having the right to touch Zia, being able to speak to her whenever he wanted. He imagined being the only man in her life. Slowly, the unyielding rigidity of tension in his shoulders and spine eased.

He refused to accept that he was falling for the Princess of Upper Mandovia because he'd never been in love in his life. He'd been in lust and he'd been infatuated and both conditions had worn off fast. He wasn't sure he even believed in love between a man and a woman, at least, *lasting* love. He had watched his parents' once-happy marriage disintegrate on the rocks of his father's cheating and his mother's endless volatile scenes. It was hard for him to believe in the longevity of a committed relationship and yet, Fiero had been with Allie for years and they were one of the happiest couples he knew. And not the only ones, he conceded grudgingly.

Immaculate once again, Zia returned to socialising in the grand ballroom, where she encountered Orazio's searing appraisal from across the room. When he unleashed his dazzling smile on her, she smiled back. And that quickly she was making up her mind to do exactly what she wanted to do…deciding that, just for once, she would embrace that luxury.

Choices had never been hers to make before. Other people had always got to make those choices for her. She hadn't even chosen to return to Mandovia for her own benefit. Once again a choice had been made for her and she had agreed because it had been the least worst option. Only now she was an adult and she needed for the sake of her own pride to behave like one.

From here on out, she would make her own decisions, regardless of whether or not they posed a risk. She was fed up with always being sensible, mature and cynical, of denying herself outlets that other, more adventurous women took for granted. Almost certainly, a couple of foolish choices could not subject her to more hurt than she had already endured in her life.

Having reached that decision, she felt positively light and airy, only abstractedly recalling all the moral lectures Alina had carefully aimed at her even while Sandrine had been partying with one man after another below the same roof. But then, to be fair, Alina was a maiden lady, who had been raised in a different era for women, an age when women were only truly valued for their virtue.

Zia had disagreed with that outlook even as a teenager and had defined her own morals as she'd grown up into a much simpler and more liveable version. Only the possibility of having a regular man in her life hadn't developed, mainly because she lacked a social life and friends to go out with. Most evenings she had been studying, attending a class, working for Sandrine or looking after Alina. In fact, her one and only experience with a member of the opposite sex had proved disappointing and distinctly frightening, she conceded with a chilled shiver of remembrance, and that had put her off pursuing more extensive experimentation.

But Orazio was a *very* safe option for her, she acknowledged thoughtfully. He didn't want any public connection to be made between them. He was only after a discreet fling. Why did that make her feel hurt? Wasn't that the same as she wanted too? It didn't mean that either of them was thinking less of the other or being disrespectful, she told herself. It would simply be a physical thing, a private thing between them alone and absolutely nobody would ever know about their more intimate moments but the two of them.

Giancarlo was glued to her side as the event ran to a close and it was becoming tedious. His persistence was becoming irritating. He talked up a storm about seeing her again, taking her out places, introducing her to his posh mates, and she listened and smiled, gently mentioning her packed itinerary over the coming weeks. But that still wasn't enough to dent Giancarlo's enthusiasm as he pointed out that she would be able to see him at quite a few of the same events. She tried not to wince at the reminder.

She went up to bed, tired but buoyed up by her plans

to be with Orazio at least once. She was embarrassed that she had not reciprocated in any way in that storage cupboard. That didn't sit well with her. Indeed it only reminded her of her comparative lack of sexual experience and made her aware that she would have to think out of the box and push herself forward, rather than wait for him to make another move.

Why on earth had she told him that she would only agree to a relationship when she didn't want one either? The complexities of her own brain bewildered her. She had been trying to hold him at bay, protecting herself in a knee-jerk reaction by rejecting him even though there was really no need for her to do that with Orazio.

While Zia agonised about what she had said and what she had not done, Orazio fell into bed, reliving the encounter in the storage cupboard, recalling her fire and her glorious responsiveness with a pained groan of fierce hunger. He would have to be subtle, he decided, and *she* didn't have a subtle bone in her body… His immediate future, nonetheless, shone like the bright heat of the sun on his horizon.

CHAPTER SIX

MID-MORNING THE NEXT DAY, Zia and Orazio with Fiero in tow set out for the border between Upper and Lower Mandovia, which was currently marked only by a sign. She had to pose at a mountain viewpoint a few yards from the border for an official photograph and then they drove for miles to the country house her mother had often visited at weekends. Apparently, a small part of it was a museum now dedicated to her mother's memory.

'We're staying the night there and moving on to the capital, Acossia, for the celebration event tomorrow. The party's being staged in the palace your father built, which is now a trendy hotel.'

'I doubt if I'll remember anything,' Zia confided. 'Young children don't really look at their surroundings much—'

'Something here might feel familiar,' Orazio remarked, covering her hand where it had fisted tautly on her knee with his. 'I should mention that the country house is also the location of a shrine to commemorate your mother. She's buried in the house chapel.'

Tensing, Zia nodded in silence, having no further comment to make on that topic. All she knew was that her mother had tried to escape over the border and a border guard from Lower Mandovia had shot her dead when she supposedly refused to identify herself. Zia didn't blame anyone, alive or dead. She reckoned tensions must've been very high at the border when Upper Mandovia was in the grip of a civil war and her unfortunate mother must've been desperate and frightened that, as the dictator's widow, she would not be accepted as a refugee.

The house sat drowsing at the end of a long driveway, a sleepy Italianate building with an elegant façade, but still very much a rural property with its worn terracotta roof tiles and simple gardens planted with clumps of mature trees and shrubs. Something stirred in the back of her mind but she quickly suppressed it, unsure that she even wanted to recall anything more from back then.

The custodian showed them round the little museum first. There wasn't much to see, faded photos, not one of which contained her late father. A bible and a few other small mementos that had reputedly belonged to her mother featured, and several very dated-looking costumes belonging to her were part of the exhibits. A beautiful black ball gown sat in a glass case and suddenly memory bit sharply into Zia and she remembered touching the dress with the glistening jewels and saying, 'You look pretty, Mummy.' Her throat closed over and her eyes stung and swam with sudden tears.

Raz guided her outside to see the shrine and her tears began drying up because that fantasy stone figure in her Greek goddess-like gown with glamorously flying long hair bore no resemblance whatsoever to the late

Princess Vittoria, who had been a very conventional, prim young woman, and Zia almost let herself down with an inappropriate laugh. She dug a tissue from her bag and dabbed at her wet eyes and cheeks even as a photographer stepped forward to capture what she had assumed was a private moment.

As Orazio moved to forestall that invasion, she stayed him with her hand on his sleeve and said, 'It's all right. This is a historic occasion and I don't mind because I lost her too. I'm not ashamed to grieve for my mother and what might've been.'

To ensure their comfort, Raz had brought staff with them, comprising a driver, a chef and a maid to manage her clothes. She was shown upstairs to her bedroom while he was handling official business. Aware she would be in the country house for only one night, her maid had packed lightly and her wardrobe of fancy outfits had been sent ahead of her to the capital. She had the evening off and she was determined to make the most of it, shedding her formal dress and pulling on jeans and a light top to go off and explore before dinner.

She found her old bedroom on the floor above, a little girl's room all painted in pink with frilly bedding and drapes. It felt vaguely familiar but as she wandered, peering into rooms that were a snapshot in time and clearly no longer used, the one place that sparked actual memories was the house chapel. Her skin turned clammy as she relived being told to sit still and stay quiet during the Mass. Her mother had been very devout. She lit a candle in her memory and read the wording on the brass plaque that adorned her late parent's ornate tomb. Her eyes swam again and she dashed the tears away irritably. There was no point thinking about how very different her life would've been had the late Princess survived and managed to join them in London.

'I wondered where you'd be hanging out,' Orazio remarked, sinking down on the worn pew beside her. 'Sorry, am I interrupting you? Were you praying?'

'No, just remembering stuff, but I've done enough of that for one day,' she said chokily.

'I'm an idiot. It didn't occur to me until we were here that all of this coming-home stuff would be very emotional for you, *piccola mia*.' He slid an arm round her shoulders and gave her a gentle squeeze before releasing her again.

For a split second she drank in the scent of him that close and gooseflesh peppered her bare arms, a sliding arrow of heat pushing up from between her legs. He smelled wonderful to her, still like a forest on an icy night, woodsy with a dash of something spicy or smoky. She turned her head and stretched up to kiss him without an ounce of hesitation. It just felt so right in that moment that she could not have resisted that urge.

Orazio jerked in surprise and then took over, both arms banding round her to crush her up against him. He nipped at her full lower lip, sent his tongue delving into the moist interior of her mouth and took her lips with hungry urgency for the barest of moments before drawing back from her again. 'Once again, this is not the place,' he quipped, scorching green eyes welded to her hectically flushed face. 'And I thought you preferred me to keep my distance.'

'Life's too short for that,' Zia framed shakily. 'I want to take advantage of every joyful moment…so, tonight, there are no rules for us. It's quiet here. If we wait until it's late, we can sneak around…'

Holding his lean, chiselled features still in receipt of that startling invitation was a challenging feat of no mean order for Raz. His love of the absurd, however, saved him from giving her a little shake of reproof and telling her that he didn't sneak anywhere, never had, never would. 'You changed your mind,' he said instead. 'Lady's prerogative.'

'*Only* for tonight,' she whispered back. 'We have to be careful and discreet.'

'You don't know a lot about passion, do you?' he murmured huskily.

'Wait and see,' she teased, her head jerking round as she heard a movement in the doorway. One of his security team checking on him. She stood up. 'I'm going for a walk round the grounds.'

'The gardens aren't extensive any more. Most of the estate has since been turned over to agriculture,' Raz volunteered.

'Oh…'

'But we can still go for a walk before dinner.'

It wasn't exactly a relaxing stroll with watchful men stirring below the trees and security trailing them. In truth their bodyguards might as well have been prison wardens, she reflected ruefully. Only behind a closed and locked door were she and Orazio free to do as they liked. Her blood fizzed through her veins as she tasted the truth that, for once, she had been bold and she had invited him to her bed. She was proud that she had had the courage, had risen above all that social conditioning that sought to deny her sex of power and agency.

Orazio was still inwardly laughing over that conversation in the church. *One night only.* She was insane if she thought she could put a lid on such an explosive attraction and shut it away again, but then there was a naivety about Zia even though she had denied that she was an innocent. If she wanted to seize every joyful moment, he would be right by her side assisting in that goal. He found her courage priceless, her utter lack of sophistication charming and her candour, a pearl beyond price.

Zia showered and donned a loose, casual summer dress because she was feeling very self-conscious and she didn't want to look vampy, as if she had planned to issue that invitation…even though she had pretty much planned it before she went to sleep the night before. Reckoning that the understaffed country house was the best location for their encounter had been only the first step, cornering him the second, speaking plainly and unambiguously about the terms the third and final step.

Her first encounter with a man had been uniformly disappointing but she was much closer to Raz and she wanted him much more than she had ever wanted anyone, important points that she had ignored when she was an impatient teenager, in a hurry to lose her innocence. She wasn't worried that Raz would hurt or shock her and she had faith that his sexual experience would ensure that their intimacy was, at the very least, unthreatening.

Fiero fielded Orazio's phone calls during the meal and ate one-handed. As the coffee was being served, he stood up and announced that he had an old friend to visit in the neighbourhood and that he would be late back.

'Did you *tell* him?' Zia asked, suspicious of that timely outing.

'Of course not.' Orazio slanted her a reproving look and she reddened. 'Although we can trust him if he were to guess because he respects boundaries.'

'I suppose you've known each other so long, that's understandable.' Zia leant across the table and whispered in the merest breath of sound, 'How do we organise this?'

Raz dealt her a slanting grin, green eyes glittering with irreverent amusement as he pictured her sitting with a time sheet and carefully slotting him in for his one allowed joyful moment. He only hoped he could live up to her expectations. 'I'll take care of it.'

'I've told my maid I'm having an early night,' she whispered again, rising from her seat and saying like a very well-trained little girl, 'Goodnight, Your Majesty.'

'Goodnight, Your Highness,' Orazio murmured gravely, watching her bright eyes dance with secretive merriment. 'Sneaking around', in her terminology, clearly gave her a buzz.

It was only half past nine but they had an early start and a long drive in the morning to reach the capital, Acossia. They could've flown in direct but more people would see them if they passed by in a car, and she appreciated that Raz could have left her to visit the house and make that drive alone, joining her only for the highlights of her trip. But both governments wanted to use the symbolism of them as a couple even if it was solely a show of a unity that wouldn't ever become real.

Orazio knocked on the door between their interconnecting bedrooms, those being the principal bedrooms in the house, and smiled at her naivety. He assumed there was a lock on her side of the door and, a moment later, he laughed as a lock turned and the door swung open and she looked up at him in astonishment, her diminutive figure clad in shorts and tee shirt, her face scrubbed clean. 'Our rooms are joined?'

'*Sì, piccola mia.* Us getting cosy is what the powers that be want,' he pointed out gently. 'Why do you think I'm along for this trip?'

Zia winced and set her teeth together. 'Those hopes make me very uncomfortable—'

'Why should they? We are still free to make our own choices.' Entirely at his ease, Orazio closed a hand over hers and led her into his bedroom, which was rather more grand, with its canopied four-poster bed, and less frilly then her own although it was still a little antiquated. She glanced at him, ridiculously self-conscious now that she actually had him in a bedroom and within close reach of a bed.

Good grief, he was drop-dead gorgeous half naked, she savoured, her mouth running dry, her breathing speeding up. Bare-chested, he wore only a pair of loose pyjama pants. He was all lean, honed muscle, a sprinkle of golden chest hair accentuating the well-developed pecs below his broad shoulders, a V-shaped band of muscle disappearing below his waistband. Her skin heating, she glanced away, awkward about the arrangement she had made. It felt too cut and dried, too organised.

And then, without any warning, Raz swept her gently up into his arms and deposited her on the big bed, where she gazed up at him with startled violet-blue eyes.

He eased up next to her, faint challenge in his narrowed emerald-green eyes. 'I want to see you naked,' he admitted thickly. 'I've wanted to see you naked from the first moment I saw you on the deck of my yacht.'

Shock and surprise hurtled through Zia. She had never been willingly naked in front of anyone since childhood. An unfortunate experience in the teenaged years had made her very cautious and she sat up, glancing warily around her. 'Are there any cameras in here?' she asked tautly.

Raz blinked in bewilderment and studied her. 'Are you joking? My security team check every room I occupy before I enter it. They're always alert to that sort of threat.'

Her rigid spine loosened a little and she breathed again. 'I had a bad experience once…'

'You'll have to tell me about that,' Orazio drawled with a frown, slipping off the bed to doff his pyjama pants without the slightest hint of inhibition.

It was a challenge. She could feel her skin warming as she saw his arousal, in effect, as it happened, her first proper glimpse of an aroused male. In an abrupt movement, she grasped the hem of her pyjama top and whipped it off over her head, determined not to act like a shy little girl. Of course, there were no cameras, nothing that could be a threat to her or her reputation because, naturally, Raz couldn't run that risk either. Momentarily, she wondered if what had happened to her had almost happened to him, but perhaps his wealth and security protection had kept him cocooned and safe from those keen to take sleazy advantage of his status.

'I'm sure you know it already, but you have the most beautiful breasts,' Orazio said half under his breath.

Zia sat up straighter, resolute in her goal to be strong, calm and confident, which she had never learned to be in the bedroom. As she met his black long-lashed green eyes, her body hummed as if an engine had suddenly switched on. The sheer heat of his appreciative gaze on her bare breasts made her nipples pebble into tight, straining points that tingled.

Raz moved closer, drawn like a magnet to the allure of those pale, perfect mounds crowned with erect brown nipples. He was in a high state of excitement absolutely new to him. This was no normal slaking of lust for him, a one-night stand, meaningless, forgettable. This was Zia and the sheer magnificent opulence of her curvaceous body. He came down over her and covered her mouth with his own, long fingers winding into her silky, lustrous hair.

'You're a great kisser,' Zia told him a few minutes later, pausing to snatch in a breath, violet eyes brilliant with desire.

'A lot of practice,' Raz quipped, gazing down at her with a sizzling smile. 'How many guys have you kissed?'

'Not as many as there should've been. I didn't have the opportunities,' she admitted ruefully. 'It was only guys I met at the hotel when I was working.'

'You were deprived of so much.'

'I bet that you got to go to adolescent parties that were unbelievably sophisticated,' she guessed.

'Guilty as charged,' he admitted, working a sizzling path down the slope of her neck to her breasts, hands rising to shape the firm, soft flesh with a rumble of pleasure. 'I was totally spoiled. I lost my innocence at thirteen.'

'Wow,' she sighed, her spine straightening as his mouth followed his caressing hands and sensation began to rise. 'I was almost eighteen…through lack of opportunity.'

'And the lucky guy was…?'

'None of your business, but he was the *wrong* guy,' she admitted, her delicate features freezing at the recollection.

'I'm incurably curious,' Orazio confided, dabbing featherlight kisses over her troubled face in an affectionate move that surprised her and she took comfort from it, even though she told herself that she shouldn't.

He returned his attention to her breasts, closing his lips round a pouting peak, crossing between that point and the other, stoking an ever-growing heat lower down in her body. He peeled off her shorts. She began to squirm, her slim length reacting to the stimulation as he slowly, carefully worked his attention down her body. And without the faintest hint of what was ahead, he bent his head, parted her thighs and ran his tongue along her cleft where she was hottest and wettest. Her spine arched and she panted out loud in surprise.

He knew the exact pressure, the perfect hot spot, and as she writhed and a long finger slid into her tight sheath, increasing the aching sensitivity at her core, she flung her head back in bliss and decided to go with the flow. Her thighs trembled, her heart pounded. Her hands sank into tousled caramel hair and clasped, fingers digging deep, her body rising and reaching higher than ever before. And then the world turned white below her lowered eyelids and she was flying into space, crying out in a blissful climax that shattered her.

Raz leant over her and crushed her parted lips fierily under his. 'We're good together,' he told her fiercely.

Zia dealt him a dazed look and lowered her lashes again, self-protection moving in to take over fast, marshalling her brain cells back into working order. As he sat up, she lifted her hands and pressed him back against the pillows. '*My* turn,' she stressed.

Orazio wasn't used to anyone, aside from himself, taking charge in the bedroom. He tensed as she pressed light kisses across his torso, ran a seeking hand down over his flexing stomach to trace his thick length, marvelling at the size of him and the velvety smooth skin before she lowered her head, her little pink tongue flicking across his crown, exciting a disconcerted groan from his parted lips. And in his head, he was picturing for every second the very first time that he saw her and, although it wasn't cool and not at all in tune with his image of himself, she was blowing his mind. His hips flexed and he arched away from her.

'I want to finish inside you,' he husked, long fingers smoothing her hair where it lay rumpled on her shoulder.

And she went red as fire and flipped over onto her back like a woman preparing herself to be a sacrifice. Once again, Zia confounded him. He didn't know what to expect, what to think because she was bold one moment but almost timid and submissive the next.

'Do you want me?' Orazio prompted with a frown

a moment later, sliding over her but making no further move.

'Why would you ask me that?' Zia snapped almost angrily.

'Because you give me mixed signals and I need to be sure that you want more,' he breathed in a raw undertone. 'You don't exactly look as if you're expecting to enjoy this.'

'Well, I didn't the first time,' she told him waspishly. 'But give me the credit to hope that you can do better!'

His brilliant green eyes widened and glittered with possessiveness and he bent his head and kissed her breathless. 'So, you tell me anything you don't like... *immediately...*'

A little of Zia's tension evaporated at that encouraging instruction and the liquid heat in her belly dissolved her growing tension. 'I've never wanted anyone the way I want you,' she admitted grudgingly.

'But then, by the sound of it, you didn't get too many choices,' he reminded her wryly. 'Am I only the latest best candidate?'

'No...' Her hand stole up without her volition to trace his strong jawline, that hint of vulnerability absolute catnip for her in a male so rawly awash with confidence. Her heart squeezed tight at the warmth of his expression.

'No, there hasn't been anyone who grabbed my interest since the wrong guy,' she confessed, because he deserved that level of honesty.

Lifted by that assurance, Raz covered her parted lips with his own again, claiming her in the most basic way possible, attuned to her every reaction, feeling the loosening of her tense muscles, the renewed melting of her slight body under his. She had been burned as he had been when he was much younger.

Zia was in heaven, her body reawakening to warm sensation, the hunger sliding back in like a greedy roar deep down inside her. She didn't know how Raz did it but he chased away her fears, made her feel safe, turned what they were sharing into a time-out-of-time encounter that required no further judgement or worry. And she needed that, she really, *really* needed that to relax, to let her body just follow the messages in anticipation of his. Until that moment, she hadn't realised she had been so traumatised by that first crushing betrayal of trust.

Orazio shifted over her, desperate to know exactly what had made her so apprehensive but knowing that it wasn't the right time to press her. Zia had her secrets as he had his and he respected that limit. He looked down at her, at the blown pupils that revealed her arousal in her lovely face, and she was breathtaking. He could not imagine a male stupid enough to risk harming or hurting her. And yet there had clearly been one.

Zia stretched up and connected with Orazio's mesmerising mouth for herself. Every time, he hit her like an illegal drug and she loved that, loved that he could take her out of her tight, judgemental self. He stilled the anxiety, soothed the still stinging wounds edging down her spine like a frightening storm warning. He was the closest she had got to a guy in five years and that bothered her because she felt she should've been stronger than that, should've moved on from that frightening first time to other, more normal men…only it hadn't happened. Opportunity and her distrust had been the barriers.

As Raz surged against her burning core, she arched her back, wanting, needing for the first time in so long. She had not felt that same burning desperation the first time. It had been a momentary need, nothing deeper or more lasting. But Raz turned her inside out with longing. She met those glittering green eyes of his and she turned liquid. She had reacted the same way the first time she'd met him in the flesh and she would never tell him that she had retained the double-page spread of him in his coronation robes a few years earlier. Back then, it had seemed harmless, a little bit of Mandovian history, nothing personal. Only now it felt to her as though things were getting very, very personal and that worried her…

Orazio surged into her with a feverish groan of satisfaction and pleasure seized her immediately, her body adjusting in the most sensual manner to his invasion, stretching to send a shock wave of sensation through her lower body. She *liked*. There was none of the pain or discomfiture that had distinguished her first encounter, no putting her in what had, with hindsight, obviously been the preferred porn position of the day. And not to put it mildly, it had hurt and that was when she had twisted round, intending to tell her partner, and instead had glimpsed the camera flickering a light out of the ajar wardrobe door.

Orazio, however, sank into her as though he had always belonged there, only she hadn't known it. Her body, damp and liquid with desire, accommodated him and the shot of intense sensation and excitement took her entirely by surprise. He moved, lean hips flexing forward, and she saw stars and constellations. It was nothing like she had ever imagined and a hundred times better than the hottest fantasy. Her body liquefied and she melted and it only got better after that as the force of his movements jolted and shifted her into full, unashamed partnership. Her body sang with wild pleasure, her heart pounded, her temperature rocketing as his fierce, urgent thrusts drove her into a shattering orgasm.

In the aftermath, she lay shell-shocked in a sublime state of relaxation, finally understanding what sex *could* be all about. Raz reached completion with a groan, his lean, powerful length shuddering over hers and then slumping briefly before he shifted his weight off her and pulled her back into the shelter of his big, powerful body.

His lazy affection afterwards made her want to curl into him even closer and she was bothered by that, perceiving clinging vibes from herself and instantly rebelling against that chilling idea to pull away. No, she was finally having her first ever one-night stand and she wasn't attaching strings or expectations to the experience, she told herself, pulling away even though she wanted to wrap herself in him as though he were a warm rug on a cold night. Those promptings unnerved her. Attachment, she had always assumed, didn't come into such encounters.

Orazio had never been pushed away before, but Zia snaked back from him as though bodily contact were toxic in the aftermath of intimacy. Anger in the face of that outright rejection stirred in his chest but he tamped it down, not wishing to come on too strong with a woman who valued her freedom to such an extent. He jumped out of bed to dispose of the protection he had used and climbed back in thirty seconds later.

Zia was a novel experience for him and, in a weird way, he was enjoying the uniqueness of having to chase rather than being pursued. She didn't want strings but he would have happily handcuffed and chained her stubborn, independent self to his bed in the royal palace. But that was where the subtlety came in, he reminded himself. He would wait until *she* appreciated what they had…

Zia disconcerted him at that point in his measured reflections by slipping out of bed with the fluidity of an eel. 'Well, that was very nice,' she told him in an upbeat tone. 'Thanks, and now that we've got all *that* out of the way, we'll be fine together and perfect as friends.'

Raz sat up in the bed in an abrupt movement. Powerful muscles rippled and tightened across his taut torso as he stared at her in undisguised wonderment while she slid agilely back into her shortie pyjamas. *Nice? Thanks?*

'I couldn't do friends,' he declared in a raw undertone. 'I don't have sex with friends.'

'But we won't be having sex again,' she pointed out unevenly, knocked wildly off balance by his statement that he could no longer be her friend. In fact that announcement made her feel as if the roof had fallen in on her and the very ground below her feet were vanishing even faster.

'I could have sex again with you right now,' Raz admitted, struggling to hang onto his temper. 'And probably tomorrow and the next day and the day after that.

I still want you now as much as I wanted you *before* you got into this bed.'

Zia frowned in bewilderment. 'But that wasn't the deal we made—'

'*What* deal?' Raz demanded, shimmering emerald eyes clinging to her flushed porcelain face in grudging fascination.

Exasperation flashed into her stormy blue eyes. 'We agreed on one night together and then that would be that—'

Raz flung his head back, tousled caramel hair gleaming in the low lights against his bronzed, chiselled features. 'I didn't agree to any such thing! I agreed to sharing what you referred to as a joyful moment. Evidently, that was no exaggeration because you've barely been with me an hour and you're *already* leaving.'

Taken aback by the smouldering vibes of sarcasm he now emanated, Zia swallowed hard. 'I thought that's what we both wanted—'

'When did you decide that *you* knew better than me about what *I* want?' he shot at her wrathfully.

The flash of unhidden anger in his bright green eyes froze her feet to the faded rug she stood on and startled her because, as a rule, Orazio appeared to be the calmest guy on the planet. Just at that instant she wouldn't have been surprised had white-hot lightning flashed through his gaze and she immediately lost ground inside herself, and felt destabilised. For years she had kept the peace for herself and Alina by avoiding conflict with Sandrine. That outlook, that lowering truth, had not equipped her very well to deal with anyone's anger.

Her mouth ran dry. 'I didn't. I assumed we both understood what *this*…' with a vague hand she indicated the mussed bed sheets '…would entail and the limits.'

'But you took the limits off last night in that storage room we were in. You told me to step away from you or step up to the plate,' Orazio reminded her very drily. 'Well, here I am and I'm doing it, I'm stepping up. I want a relationship with you. I'm not sneaking around anywhere…that is *not* me. We're both single. We can be together openly if we want to be and you still haven't explained why we *can't* be.'

Shock was reverberating through Zia like a giant bell suddenly clanging above her head, drowning out her own hopelessly confused inner voices. Yes, she had said that to him, she recalled dimly, throwing down the challenge but *never* expecting him to pick it up. She had never been in a relationship with a male before and the very prospect, she registered belatedly, *terrified* her. She didn't let anyone in. She didn't let anyone get close. Her circle of trust extended to only herself. That was how she kept herself safe and it had been like that for many more years than she cared to recall.

Her mother had first broken her trust by disappearing and Sandrine had soon followed and then, more sadly, Alina, when she had finally grasped that Alina might be an adult but that she was a powerless one without a voice. Nobody had come to save that battered and bruised little girl when she'd cried in her bed at night, nobody had intervened or *cared*, and that lesson still lingered with Zia even now that she was grown up.

In the present, determined not to expose her vulnerability to that extent, Zia forced her spine straight and stood tall. 'I genuinely believed we were agreeing to just one night together and I was fine with that but, obviously, you're not. I'm sorry we've had this misunderstanding,' she continued glibly on the way to the door back to her own room.

'Zia!' Orazio growled raw and low. 'Don't you dare walk away from me without explaining yourself.'

Zia half turned her head, stinging tears washing the backs of her eyes. 'Raz, I—'

'Is there someone else back in London?' he cut in.

'No… I wouldn't have been with you tonight if there were,' she muttered.

'But you don't trust me…right?'

'It's no reflection on you,' she murmured with perceptible regret. 'I just don't trust *anybody*. It's best we return to being hands-off with each other, healthier for both of us to accept that this just can't work out.'

'You don't know me well enough yet, but I assure you,' Raz breathed in a driven undertone, 'I could *make* it work—'

But she still ran like a rabbit with a fox on its tail, Raz thought furiously, back into her own room, lock immediately snapped shut again. She wouldn't even fight with him and the surprise of that, with her combative character, held him still for long moments while he tried to work out what had gone wrong, what he had said or done that had roused her to that attitude.

CHAPTER SEVEN

'ZIA WILL BURN out soon,' Fiero forecast in a grim whisper three weeks later. 'What will the governments do then? Nobody's acknowledging the amount of work she's accomplishing, the pressure she's under, the *stress* of it all. But you understand it better than anyone. Why aren't you urging her to take a weekend off?'

Orazio breathed in deep and slow. As usual he had barely taken his attention off Zia for a second, watching her work her way round various children, stooping down to join in their pursuits with a level of success he could never have equalled. It was no wonder that the population of *his* country, Lower Mandovia, was already complaining about being deprived of exposure to the already renowned Princess.

Upper Mandovia had taken to Zia like ducks to water. She was everywhere and always the focus of adoring, fascinated crowds. If there was a hospice, a hospital, a school or a nursery or a dog rescue facility, they were begging for a visit. Patients, the sick and the dying, children, animals—she had all the compassion he had never managed to produce. The natural touch, he had labelled it, that unending smile and acceptance, that ability to empathise in the worst possible situations. But in every way her instincts were innate and she was entirely herself, which he hugely admired. It wasn't studied, it wasn't a learned approach—it galled him, but it came as part of her.

'So, am I allowed to ask what went wrong that night at the country house when just being around the two of you felt like being a very large, surplus gooseberry?' his best friend enquired ruefully.

Orazio breathed in deep. 'It went wrong,' he acknowledged wryly.

'So, think simple. You take it back there and do it differently,' Fiero suggested in an awkward undertone because, as a rule, he never interfered and never ever offered advice.

'I *can't*,' Orazio confided simply. 'She rejected me. I was ditched, first time ever…no jokes, please.'

Fiero sucked in his breath sharply at that admission. 'But you could still suggest that she needs a break—'

'She doesn't need me to do that. Right now, *here*, I'm just the support act,' Orazio breathed with a slightly bitter edge.

'OK,' his best friend acknowledged without any expression at all.

The newspapers had given up hoping for signs of intimacy between them, Raz reflected ruefully. The media had surrendered their fantasy romance in despair at their failure as a couple to meet their countries' fond hopes. They had openly declared the polite, unemotional state of the relationship between him and Zia. He didn't touch her in any way unless there was no other choice, and she mirrored that approach. It was as if a new Ice Age had sprung up between them. There was no hint of intimacy or friendship, indeed there was *nothing*. A sort of chilly indifference invaded her when he got close, ensuring that he didn't get too familiar, that he knew that any attention would be unwelcome.

Across the room, Zia scrambled upright again, perspiring from her efforts in joining in with the toddlers' finger painting, knowing her clothing bore stains, knowing she had probably made an ass of herself again but refusing to care. All Zia knew was that she had never been more unhappy in her life. She worked through every day in a blind state of misery, grateful to have other stuff to concentrate on.

Somehow, she had fallen *insanely* in love with Orazio. The morning after they had gone to bed, when there was a positive chill in the air over breakfast, she had looked at him and finally understood with a piercing pain inside her just how deep her feelings for him already ran. Every inch of her had longed for that intimacy to be reinstated, every fibre of her being had longed for the return of their shared glances of understanding and the carefully hidden moments of mutual amusement. It had been an intimacy that had gone far beyond sex. Why had she realised that only when it was too late to change anything? Indeed, the pain of loving Orazio crashed up against her defences every time she attempted to deny it.

Removing even her attention from his drop-dead gorgeous person was a challenge and every night she lay in her bed remembering how it had felt when they were *together*. In the daylight, those memories felt unreal because, right now, they were further apart than they had been the very first day they had met. Yet this was the guy she *loved.* And the love had happened, regardless of whether she wanted it or not. And she hadn't wanted it, hadn't ever wanted to put her emotional stability in the hands of a male. Yet there it was and he had offered her *more* and what had she done?

She had turned him down.

The guy who was so kind, so honourable, so honest with her that he had even been frank about his own intentions. He had supported her, protected her, even from her own mistakes, from their first meeting.

And in the intervening weeks, horribly deprived of him, denied even the regular phone calls that she had adored, coming to terms with just how much she craved his company and his counsel, she had slowly come to understand *why* she had fled what he had offered her. She hadn't loved anybody since her mother had vanished from her life and she had worked hard to ensure that she had no expectations of anyone who had followed. Because there had been nobody. And now she *loved* Orazio and it was frightening: all of her felt as though she were composed of raw, very sensitive nerve endings. His every move controlled her and she was fighting all those impulses to run away again in spite of the fact that she had chased him off.

And why had she done that?

In a nutshell: it hurt to love and lose. And she was an emotional coward because she had never known a successful relationship born out of love. Her mother had simply disappeared from her life and it had been years before she had finally learned that her unfortunate mother had died. The wound of her mother's vanishing act had never really healed. And that had been followed by the people she had cared for regrettably letting her down, failing to protect her, failing to meet her needs. But she knew that she needed to move on from that isolationist stance. How could she ever find happiness if she trusted only herself? Was she planning to stay alone for ever?

And yet *he* had said that he could *make* it work between them.

Wasn't it horribly, inexcusably cowardly of her to not even have given him that chance?

Particularly when he wouldn't even be around her for much longer, she reflected miserably. After all, as the days had moved into weeks, it had been impossible for even governmental wishes to prevent Orazio from having to fly back and forth to take care of his own duties in Lower Mandovia. Already, he was only present to share main events with her and this evening there was a big party being thrown in her late father's ghastly gilded former palace at which they would both appear together. *Together?* That was a bit of a joke when they could barely manage a civil conversation.

And whose fault was that? Solely *hers*, she acknowledged wretchedly, knowing she had rejected him out of fear alone. What normal male would wish to continue being saddled with her company in those circumstances? She needed to cross the barrier between them that she had imposed. She needed to speak to him and tell him the truth and do it soon.

Zia pulled a face at her image in the full-length mirror in front of her. Cream in shade in a glittering ball gown, very flattering, accentuating her small waist and curvier attributes above and below, and what did it matter? Another photo opportunity? Another chance to prove that she was working the role she was being paid to fulfil? Yet she had still seen not one red cent of the salary she had been promised, she conceded ruefully. Her bank account was as empty as it had ever been and she might be sporting designer fashion at the government's expense, but she remained a literal pauper beneath her fancy trappings.

Orazio watched Zia enter the ballroom as Princess Annunziata and she did it to the manner born. Tiny though she was even in heels, she exuded class and dignity. Obviously, he could only admire her for that air of panache when she had grown up in such difficult circumstances. She was solid steel strength below the intensely feminine trappings, quite unlike any woman he had *ever* met. And she was gorgeous, absolutely gorgeous, shimmering like a candle glowing in the dark, the centre of everyone's attention but, unlike many of her sex, *not* luxuriating in that attention.

He watched Giancarlo Marone head for her like a guided missile and looked away, annoyed beyond measure, annoyed he couldn't put a fist in his face and tell him to back off, urges that had never afflicted Orazio before. Somehow, she had forged him into this guy who was possessive, territorial and jealous. He despised this *new* version of himself, being all too well aware that he had no rights over Zia's body or her affections and that he would have to stand by as an unwilling captive audience to any resulting courtships. All his life he had associated the stronger emotions with his parents' hostile marriage, the anger, jealousy and hatred that had powered their volatile confrontations.

Only moments later as the event kicked off, he was thoroughly disconcerted when Zia appeared in front of him and reached for his hands as if she were drowning and hissed half under her breath, 'Dance with me. Giancarlo's a pain.'

Zia had learned how to do all the formal dances on his yacht and she moved smoothly round the floor with him while he tried and failed to compute that most unexpected invitation. He was hugely aware of the flashes of the photographers stealing photos of such a long-awaited shot of them and marvelled that she was willing to give them the opportunity when for weeks she had been treating him like a rather contagious disease she would prefer not to risk catching.

Zia looked up at him, beautiful violet-blue eyes gripping his. 'I need to talk to you.'

Orazio stilled in shock at that announcement because it was arriving more than a little late in the day, as it were. 'That will be a problem. I'm leaving in twenty minutes. I have a wedding to attend tomorrow morning back home.'

'Oh…' Zia said simply, her lovely face reddening and visibly wilting. 'I waited too long—'

'No, you didn't,' Raz hastened to assure her, although if he had been honest, he would've admitted that he had given up hope. 'But you need to give us space to be alone. You have to tell your managers that you need a break at the country house this weekend and they'll move any engagements on to another week. Nobody works seven days a week, Zia. You're entitled to time off, just like me. Haven't you worked that out yet?'

'I've always worked seven days a week,' she muttered apologetically. 'I didn't get days off.'

'You're not a maid any more than you are still at Sandrine Beccari's beck and call. Stand up for yourself. If you need a break now, you have to *ask* for it,' he emphasised.

Zia was already getting jittery at the prospect of demanding time off from her tough schedule, but if Orazio said that that was her *right*, she would go for it. Talking to him was unavoidable and she wasn't prepared to duck the necessity a second time. Not even if she was that gutless at heart. 'OK. I'll do that. I could maybe also get the chance on the Friday afternoon of going to visit Alina and see how she's doing with her sister.'

'But the rest of the weekend, you're *mine*.' Glittering green eyes gripped hers and her tummy whirled as if a thousand butterflies had been let loose, heart rate increasing, mouth running dry.

'T-to talk,' she stammered, unwilling to commit that far even though at that moment there was nothing more in that world that she wanted to be than *his*. That compelling attraction was undeniable, impossible to ignore.

'Of course…initially,' Raz dared, reading her wonderfully expressive face that had been shuttered to him for so many weeks, grasping that he was a much more impatient male than he had ever appreciated. He had expected instant acceptance, instant gratification, all the expectations of a pretty privileged, young, rich male. But she didn't work like that, on some preordained spoiled, ambitious woman timeline, and he didn't want her to change, he acknowledged helplessly, he wanted her to go on being her unique, singular self, who kept him guessing and on the edge. It excited him more than anything else with a woman ever had.

Zia retired to her room that night and employed her phone to insist that she needed a free weekend, surprised at how easy it was for scheduled events to be rescheduled once she actually requested it. Ironically, she had needed Raz to contend that it was her right to behave that way. Even though she had yet to receive a salary for her 'work', she had been treating her handlers as though they were her employers.

That Friday afternoon, she was taken up through the mountains to visit Alina. It bothered her that she was accompanied by the official photographer and she made it clear that there would be no photos without her host's permission. She was greeted on the doorstep by Alina's eldest nephew, Felipe, and ushered indoors to a stuffy parlour where she was served with a formal high tea. It was utterly foreign to Zia and she looked at Alina in helpless dismay, rising from her sofa to embrace the elderly woman as she also stood up in obvious embarrassment.

Alina squeezed her shoulder. 'This is how it *must* be. London was another world and everything is different. You are *our* Princess now,' she muttered uncomfortably.

'I'm still your Zia,' Zia whispered painfully.

'Not any more, *mi pequeña mascota*,' Alina sighed. 'My sister and I believe you will be the next Queen of Mandovia—'

'Are you crazy?' Zia exclaimed in disbelief.

Alina held the younger woman back from her and scanned her lovely face with deep affection and understanding. 'No. I think you are blind to what is happening in front of you. Right at this minute, you have a king hanging around you like a second skin and us older people understand that that means more than the show in public. A man such as he is doesn't make a show in front of others…he's too private.'

Zia's pulses kicked up at the thought that her former nurse could be right. It was true, Orazio wasn't anyone who would ever make an open demonstration of feelings. Unlike her, he was guarded, reserved. And all of a sudden, encouraged by Alina's romantic expectations, she hoped that Alina was right and that, after all, she hadn't made the wrong move in admitting that she needed to talk to him.

'We'll see,' she breathed, struggling to act non-committal, returning to her seat, switching into public mode as Alina's older sister and her family appeared to join them.

And when the meeting was over and, at the photographer's request, she asked Alina if she or her family would object to a photo being taken, she was, much to her surprise, informed that that was fine with them. They all clumped up around her outside their cottage and beamed and Zia was utterly disconcerted by their cooperation. Alina gave her a comforting hug as she departed, saying quietly, 'Zia…you're making history.'

They arrived at the country house a couple of hours later for her weekend off duty. Her staff, such as they were, her maid, her PR person, disappeared as soon as she put her foot on the gravel in front of the old house. She was feeling insanely nervous at the prospect of Orazio's descent. She had invited him, built anticipation and, really, how was she supposed to deal with that? She had no magical justification for him, had no idea whatsoever *how* to meet his expectations. Did he even *have* expectations?

And did she even know what her own expectations were? She just wanted, *needed* to be with him again without the chill of misunderstanding and distance that made her feel so alone.

Early evening moved slowly for Zia because her nerves were riding her hard. She showered and changed into a summer dress, refreshed her make-up, in fact did everything the average woman did when expecting a spectacular male to arrive. She stared out of windows, drank too much coffee, paced the floor until she heard a helicopter. She raced out onto the front lawn—no, not cool, at all—watched the heavy craft land in the meadow just past the garden boundary, swiftly followed by a second helicopter, men disembarking, spreading out, talking into ear buds. Yes, Orazio had arrived, complete with his usual security ring.

From there, she watched him vault out of the first helicopter, sheathed in a sleek navy suit teamed with a dark shirt and, for once, no tie. Almost immediately, his light gaze settled on her, eyes narrowing to focus on her, and he smiled, stalking towards her with sure strides, long, powerful legs negotiating the low fence that lay between the meadow and the garden with ease. Her heart bounced inside her chest so hard that she was breathless.

'I brought my chef with food for us,' he announced before he even reached her.

Her expressive face fell. 'I didn't even think of food,' she admitted ruefully. 'But I could've cooked for us.'

'Our personal agenda is more important,' Raz informed her, closing an arm round her tense shoulders to herd her back indoors and straight into the old-fashioned drawing room to one side of the hall. 'So, let's talk.'

Not surprisingly that invitation silenced Zia, because she had never before met an actual male who was that eager to 'talk'. Fingers sliding tautly together, she suggested he sit down, but Orazio was too focused on her to listen, his shrewd green eyes running down her slight figure and back up again with a measured intensity that set every nerve cell in her body twanging with awareness.

'I want to feel your mouth under mine again, *piccola mia*,' he told her frankly. 'I can barely wait.'

A little quiver shimmied through her entire body, lighting up places that hadn't awakened since their stay in the house a month earlier. Her breasts swelled and the peaks tightened into almost painful tingling buds and a sliding liquid sensation invaded between her thighs. 'Er…' she mumbled, totally out of her depth with this forceful sexual male.

Orazio hitched a black brow. 'OK?'

Zia nodded frantically, registering that he was asking her permission, which felt ridiculous to her in that moment when her every skin cell craved a closer connection with him. It was as though an electrical storm broke out when her eyes collided with his. It wiped out her thoughts, sent her body into pure reaction, was almost more than she could bear with any equanimity because all of it encompassed what she had sworn never to feel again around a male: that heady, utterly intoxicating pull of wild attraction. And Orazio hit every button in her body and her brain with terrifying accuracy.

He pulled her close and lifted her up to him and virtually devoured her mouth with a passion that lit her up inside like a burning torch. It was as though he had lit a touch paper to a stick of dynamite because suddenly she was fully on board, hands rising to dig into that luxuriant caramel-blond hair, to hold him close, to *touch* him when she had feared that she would never have that chance again. And all her plans to stage a serious discussion simply fell apart at that point. Orazio swept her up fully into his arms and said thickly, 'We'll go upstairs…more private.'

'We were supposed to talk,' she reminded him rebelliously as he carried her bodily up the winding staircase.

'It's been almost a month… I'm *dying* for you,' he growled in objection half under his breath.

And something visceral in her thrilled to that sensual declaration. After all, she had spent most of that same month wondering and worrying what other women could be in his life, what other woman could be in his bed, pleasing him after she had walked away.

'What were we to talk about?' Orazio asked as he sloughed off his jacket and dropped it in a heap before embarking on his shirt buttons as if getting naked was the only thing on his mind.

'Why I walked away…stuff I need to explain—'

'I just want you, on *any* terms,' Orazio specified in a raw undertone, smouldering emerald-green eyes capturing her across the width of his canopied bed. 'I don't want anyone else. I *only* want you.'

And that was enough in that instant to soothe Zia's insecurity because she didn't believe that she had ever been wanted simply for herself. Her title, her heritage, meant very little to Orazio, born royal as he had been, the golden child and heir from birth of a hereditary monarchy. He had never needed to question who he was, what he was, whether he even mattered. Nobody had ever made Orazio Arcangeli feel *less* and, odd as it sometimes felt, she adored that scorching confidence of his, which was such a contrast to her own constant inner anxieties.

She began to peel her dress off over her head but he forestalled her, stalking round the bed to catch her to his lean, powerful body and say, 'Let me do it, *piccola mia*.'

The straps on her dress also fastened on the shoulders, which she had not noticed but which he had spotted, and her dress dropped to her ankles, leaving her feeling abruptly *very* exposed in her lacy, fancy lingerie, the sort of garments she had never owned in her life before coming to Mandovia.

'You are so beautiful,' Raz growled, dropping down on his knees to skim her panties down and push straight into the kind of intimacy she was disconcerted by as his lean fingers parted her thighs and he zoomed in on the tender space between.

Her legs trembled under her as he homed in on the most sensitive spot of all. Only halfway out of his shirt, which still hung unbuttoned, Orazio was on his knees in front of her, lean hands parting her thighs, long fingers occasionally stroking.

'We were supposed to talk…and yet here we are,' Zia framed, shaking now like a leaf in the storm, fierce sensation darting through her with every circle of his lips near her aching bud, every invasive probe from his fingers.

Orazio flicked a glance up at her, barely pausing in

his sensual ministrations to her yearning body. 'This is how we should be. We can talk any time.'

And she wanted to argue but sensation was piling on sensation in a fiery lava flow of hunger. Before she knew where she was or what she was doing, she was soaring up the scale and off the planet, white flashing behind her lowered eyelids, cries she couldn't silence breaking open her lips as a shattering climax claimed her brain and her body. In the aftermath, she rested back against the wall simply to stay upright. He plucked her off the wall as if she weighed no more than a small child and shifted her to the bed, standing over her then as he removed what remained of his clothes.

'I missed you so much,' he bit out fiercely.

Zia tried and failed to regain control of her thoughts and then surrendered. 'Yes, me too,' she gasped unevenly, still struggling to catch her breath while she studied him. He was a literal vision of her ideal fantasy male, all bronzed rippling muscle and intense passion.

'Don't ever cut me out like that again,' he urged.

'Thought I was doing what I needed to do…but I was *wrong*,' Zia admitted tautly as he tugged her to him and kissed her with feverish urgency.

'We can all get stuff stuck in our heads that makes us act crazy,' Orazio told her with assurance. 'I was scared of the sheer strength of my attraction to you because lust was, I suspect, all my parents ever had.'

He could be so much more open than she was, found it so much easier to talk about such things, that she was almost unnerved because she had made such a production out of her need to *talk* to him and was *still* holding back. And then here was Orazio, giving away private stuff for free and without fuss.

His firm, sensual mouth caressed hers and his tongue delved and an inadvertent whimper escaped somewhere low in her throat as desire reignited. He tugged away her bra, moulded her breasts, toyed with the prominent tips, sucking, nibbling, stoking the slow burn of arousal starting to rise again in her pelvis. Somewhere deep down in her brain she thought about him telling her that it wasn't only sex for him with her and the physical pleasure he was giving her seemed to steadily multiply. He made her feel safe, so much safer than she had ever dared to feel with anyone.

As her hands roamed over every part of him that she could reach, he shuddered over her, his big, powerful body pressing her down into the mattress until, with a growl, he tipped her back, tipping her legs over his shoulders, and rose over her. He drove into her sensitive channel in one urgent thrust and her body jackknifed up under him on the rushing tide of pleasure seizing hold of her. It was even better than the last time because their bodies knew each other and he had the truly stunning gift of seeming to know exactly what she needed.

The urgent pace he set made the bed creak and he laughed at the noise, grinning down at her with amusement, lancing appreciation firing his green eyes. 'So we'll put a new modern bed in here—'

'Before you break this one?' she teased breathlessly.

And then he withdrew and flipped her over to place her on her knees and she suppressed the dangerous rip tide of bad memories and decided to let him make new ones for her. She closed her eyes and luxuriated in the sensual delight of his body possessing hers with vigour. A long finger teased her clit and, faster than she could have believed, she erupted into orgasm again, every muscle convulsing, every nerve cell tingling as he too reached satisfaction.

As she settled down on the bed beside him, he closed an arm round her in a sudden show of greater intimacy and for a split second she froze in denial before her tension gave. She would let herself enjoy Orazio for as long as their relationship lasted, she told herself fiercely. She needed to be all in, not half out with him, because he was too intense, too driven to do anything by halves.

Zia cuddled into him for the first time and Orazio smiled above her down-bent head, tousled black silken waves of her stunning mane of hair spread across his bare chest. He felt remarkably like a male who had conquered Everest, he conceded wryly, closing a second arm round her, breathing in the familiar fruity scent of her skin.

'And now you can tell me what we need to talk about,' he suggested.

Zia tried very hard not to freeze, not to feel challenged, in short to copy his frank ability to disclose personal stuff that she had always held onto as if it were her secret store of gold nuggets.

'I find it hard to trust,' she muttered in a nervous rush. 'The first guy I was with had a camera in his wardrobe to capture our…er…intimacy. He worked at the hotel with me and he'd heard a rumour that I was born a princess. He thought if he did a film of us in bed, he could sell it for a lot of money somewhere.'

'Disgusting,' Raz remarked without hesitation. 'What age were you?'

'Seventeen but he wasn't much older. I turned my head because he was hurting me and glimpsed the camera. I snatched it off the tripod and threatened him with the police. I didn't know my rights then, though, or the law. I panicked, took the camera with me so that he couldn't use anything he had captured. He was begging and pleading with me not to go to the police. I had no intention of going to the police,' she acknowledged. 'I was too humiliated and embarrassed by the whole set-up.'

'And that was that, you did nothing?' Orazio pressed.

'What could I do without drawing the kind of attention to my identity that I most feared? When I was younger, I was afraid that someone hurt or killed by my father's regime might come after me for revenge,' she confessed ruefully. 'I learned very young that I'm the only person that I can depend on. I have to protect myself because there's nobody else to do it.'

'No, I'll protect you now,' Orazio declared with assurance.

'You don't need to say impressive stuff like that to me. I'm not expecting it. We're just having a…a moment, a fling, whatever you want to call it,' she reasoned bravely.

'Neither of those,' Raz slotted in, contradicting her assumption calmly, his arms tightening round her. 'Any other bad experiences to share?'

'No, I didn't trust guys after that one and I didn't get close enough to anyone again,' she admitted with a wince. 'It felt like too much of a risk and a time-waster. Just surviving to make a future I could face felt like a big enough challenge.'

'I can understand that,' Raz conceded. 'But you also

have to understand and eventually *accept* that I will never fall into the unreliable category.'

'Nobody can say that about themselves,' she argued.

'I'm very consistent in temperament and attitude. If I say that you can trust me, I genuinely will never let you down,' he insisted.

Unnerved by that certainty of his, Zia took a deep breath before saying apprehensively, 'So, what next?'

'We'll go downstairs for dinner and you can reunite with that very poorly trained dog of yours, who is currently scratching against our bedroom door,' Orazio murmured smoothly.

And she was out of his arms within a split second, hurtling naked across the room to open the door and let Sausage in. Raz was grateful that he had judged that reunion correctly, deeming such gestures the building blocks of a successful relationship. His rare relaxed smile flashed out and as she glanced back at him, she was shaken by the vision of Orazio sprawled across the bed, naked but for the sheet across his lower body, incredibly relaxed and at ease with himself. That smile of his, however, could just light up her world and make her feel breathless and brainless.

'About us,' she began to specify cautiously, clutching Sausage under one arm as she clambered back into bed with him. He deemed it not the time to tell her that he wasn't intending to share his bed with his dogs or hers. When Orazio saw a challenge, he moved with infinite care towards his goal and embraced patience and tolerance. Only that had been in business, he had never had to do it with a woman in mind before, he acknowledged a shade worriedly. He suspected that both negotiations and compromises lay ahead on his path.

‘Us? Oh, that’s simple,’ Orazio stated. ‘We stop hiding. We admit we’re in a relationship. We become an official couple. It’ll cause a fuss for a week and then we’ll be left pretty much in peace.’

‘I wasn’t thinking of us going that far,’ Zia confided uncomfortably. ‘Not so soon.’

‘I don’t think it’s too soon. If we’re honest, we can then control the narrative, which is much wiser,’ he declared confidently.

CHAPTER EIGHT

'OK?' ORAZIO CHECKED in an undertone, quietly guiding Zia out onto the former palace balcony where her father, the hated dictator, had once made his grandiose public appearances.

Yet again, the politicians had picked the cleverest spot from which to make their chosen message through the appearance of the Mandovian 'royals'. She and Orazio were now linked together like salt and pepper and she marvelled that he didn't resent her for it.

'Of course,' Zia fibbed because, no, she wasn't really OK at all with the thousands of people heaving in the city square below them, cheering and waving up at them with what struck her as almost hysterical enthusiasm.

Orazio had assured her that the seemingly exciting news of their relationship would die down within a week but his forecast had been *wrong*. My word, she thought weakly as she kept her forced smile in place and stood, a small, straight figure within the shelter of the relaxed masculine arm enclosing her. *My word, had Orazio got it wrong!* The two of them being together as a couple was clearly the very biggest thrill either Upper or Lower

Mandovia had seen since the revolution that had toppled her late father from power.

For the past month, she and Orazio had had to hurtle between both countries completing engagements. And now that they were genuinely together with the reunification on the horizon, they were both in constant demand as a pair, a seemingly *indivisible* couple. The newspapers had got really silly with their articles, suggesting suitable wedding dates, the best designers for 'the dress', right down to rather offensively implying that Orazio must be none too keen on making a lasting commitment to her if he had not yet *popped the question*. It was all so unfair to him, she thought guiltily. He had so obviously *not* foreseen the complicated, deeply personal expectations that would explode in the public arena if they came out and were honest about their relationship.

They were ushered out of the palace that was now a hotel by a rear entrance where only the paparazzi knew to await their exit. A posse of security guards ringed them to hold back the crush of cameras and keep the shouted questions at a distance. Zia almost winced as she heard someone demand to know when they were getting married and it was far from the first time that that question had been asked. It still rather surprised her that Orazio hadn't just dumped her to protect himself from such aggressive demands. Nobody, it seemed, could simply let them be together without expecting their togetherness to be made swiftly official and to see her crowned as his Queen.

In opposition to Zia's anxious reflections, Orazio was thinking that everything that day, and for many days previous to it, had gone superlatively well. *His* Princess was gradually adapting to intense public exposure and surely more than ready for him to propose a permanent union. According to his reckoning, he had gone very slowly indeed and he had kept everything low-key and calm, which was the most comfortable pace for him. To his relief, his own more intense emotions had cooled down now that they were together and everybody knew it. There was no reason now for him to feel that seething jealousy or possessiveness.

From the moment he had ended up in bed with Zia he had known she would become his wife. Surely, she was now expecting a proposal? Working up to the moment as though they were some normal romantic couple would be unnecessary, he decided, everything reserved in his nature shying away from the threat of having to get emotional with anyone…*even* his intended bride.

At the airport in Upper Mandovia, they clambered into a helicopter and conversation was impossible for the duration of the flight. Fiero was in the limo that ferried them back to the castle where Zia now lived in the Queen's Tower on a more permanent basis. And only now was Zia questioning all of those facts, she realised in dismay. Poor Raz had sleepwalked into the marriage trap *with* her! He had got everything wrong while striving to show due consideration and respect to all involved parties, she reasoned in consternation.

'Zia and I want to talk,' Raz announced, reaching for her hand in such a natural move that she was completely silenced just as Harvey, his head of household, approached him for a discreet word.

Orazio's lean bronze chiselled features froze for a

fraction of a second and then he turned to look at her with a smile and murmured, 'My grandfather and my mother have arrived for an impromptu visit. I'm afraid we'll have to take a rain check on—'

Even as he spoke, a volcanic flood of Spanish erupted nearby. Zia spun round to find that a tall, impossibly elegant lady with silver hair and a fantastic number of diamonds on her person was bearing down on her with an aggressive stare. Orazio stepped between the two women and urged Zia towards the stairs. 'I'll see you shortly,' he swore.

Before Zia could start up the stone steps, a tall, lean, older man with white hair stepped into her path. 'I am Xavier Zalas, Orazio's grandfather. Please excuse his mother's outburst. Occasionally she forgets her manners. I shall look forward to getting to know you.'

It was a timely intervention and she grasped the old man's extended hand politely, flashing her signature warm smile. Even so, her ears were still ringing from hearing Orazio be verbally attacked for dating that 'loathsome man's daughter'! Even though the former Queen and Orazio's mother, Luisa Arcangeli, had lowered her voice, her shrill syllables had been unmistakeable in tone. She seemed to believe that her son was on the brink of marrying Zia and had been so horrified by that suspicion that she had flown all the way from Venezuela to make her opposition known.

'That would be lovely,' she answered his grandfather graciously before, with one flash of his expressive green eyes, Orazio sent an unmistakeable warning to her to disappear and leave him alone to deal with his difficult parent. With a sigh, already well attuned to that silent prompt of caution, Zia turned again and climbed the stairs to her room. Those tabloid rumours were causing all sorts of misunderstandings, she conceded with a heavy heart. Of course, Orazio was *not* thinking of marrying her and would doubtless soon soothe his mother's worries.

But, just as naturally, Zia was made miserable by that overheard snatch of dialogue. His mother's hostility only reminded her that she absolutely loved Orazio from the bottom of his heels to the crown of his actual head and that there was *no* future in it. How could she possibly feel any other way about him when they had spent the last month as lovers and he had supported her in every way there was? In short, even Zia knew that she adored him. Orazio had become *everything* to her. How could he be anything else? This was the guy who enfolded her in a lovers' embrace every night that he was with her. Since they had come out as a couple, nobody expected them to be apart at night, aside from the *ultra* conservatives, who took issue with them openly living together before marriage.

Yet that had not been what they had been thinking when they had done that, she acknowledged guiltily, worried that Orazio had not foreseen the likely result of the unhidden intimacy they shared…such as his family turning up to express their objections to such a connection with the dictator's daughter! She stripped in her fancy built-in dressing room and pulled on a robe to go for a shower, a well-worn routine in the evening. She would relax in a bath first and eventually rejoin Raz for dinner, just the two of them. And, naturally, reports of such constant togetherness had escaped when they had been so *open* about stuff, she reflected painfully. Doubtless that was why his relations had arrived without warning, so, there would be no such togetherness this evening.

She lay back in her bath and drifted off into thoughts about Raz. He made her happier than she had ever been in her life because, for the first time ever, she *wasn't* alone and she had someone she could truly depend on. Only their relationship wasn't going to last for ever, she reminded herself. Since the start she had decided that living strictly in the moment made the most sense. She would enjoy what they had while it lasted rather than depress herself with images of the hurt and rejection that she would experience when they broke up. She was such a dreadful pessimist. Raz tended to complain about that downbeat outlook of hers but then he had lived a very different life from her, a much safer, more secure life where literally everything he had ever wanted magically came to him.

A quick shower later, with her hair casually dried to tumble round her shoulders, her maid arrived to inform her that Orazio was waiting for her. With his family? She tried not to wince at the prospect of dining with his hostile mother and dug out a fancy dress to put on, because she had begun to enjoy the little feminine things she had never had time or reason to consider before. And Raz was very responsive to the right dress, she reflected with a wicked little grin as she outlined her lips with a foxy red shade and decided that the former Queen of Mandovia was not going to make her hang her head as though she had done something to be ashamed of.

She promenaded down the wide corridor because,

in high heels, she couldn't walk any faster, and passed on into the spacious drawing room they used, surprised that their Venezuelan guests were not already ensconced there. A bare minute later, Orazio joined her. Sheathed in the fashionable ripped jeans he often wore around her now when he was off duty, his tall, powerful body was delineated in faded denim and a khaki tee. And that fast, she couldn't take her eyes off him because she found Raz staggeringly sexy in ordinary casual clothes.

'Where's your family gone?'

'To dine with the Marone clan on their yacht in the harbour. They're old friends of my mother's and she couldn't leave fast enough once she received their invitation,' he told her with sardonic amusement. 'I didn't warn her that Giancarlo's papa has changed wives since she was last here. She'll be outraged when she finds that out.'

'That was mean,' Zia reproved.

'No less than Luisa deserves with her nonsense.'

'You call your mother by her Christian name?'

'According to her, being addressed as "mamma" is aging. I've been calling her Luisa since I was ten,' he confided, seeing her surprise at that information and raising a broad shoulder in an uneasy, embarrassed shrug before squaring his jaw. 'I owe you more of an explanation.

'My mother wasn't the most loving, caring parent,' he admitted uncomfortably. 'For all his faults, my father was better in that department and my grandfather is also a much warmer and more caring personality.'

'Are you being fair to your mother?' Zia prompted

thoughtfully. 'Or are you just annoyed right now that she arrived and said what she did?'

Orazio compressed his wide sculpted mouth before breathing in deep and wincing. 'I'm afraid that Luisa is a selfish, cold and consistently bored socialite, who should never have had a child and who probably wouldn't have bothered having one if it hadn't been necessary for the monarchy. Why do you think I'm an only child?'

'Oh…' Zia lowered her troubled gaze, scolding herself for having assumed that his childhood had been a much smoother and easier ride than hers. Now that it occurred to her, she marvelled that she hadn't immediately noticed that Luisa had made no attempt even to embrace the son that she hadn't seen in many months and, furthermore, had no problem dining with friends rather than family on her first night back in Mandovia.

'So, let's forget about our visitors for now and concentrate on us. You look…' Raz dropped his dark deep drawl low as Harvey stepped in the door carrying an ice bucket and disappeared again almost as quickly '*…delectable.*'

Green eyes collided with dark blue and her head swam and her nipples tightened and that familiar ache of longing between her thighs kicked up a storm. She snatched in a shortened breath as Orazio reached for her and lifted her up into his arms, striding over to an opulent velvet couch to drop down on it with Zia arranged across his thighs.

'I hate it when I can't touch you all day. It's an unbelievable torment,' he confided huskily, long fingers reaching up to comb softly through her silky hair and tug her head up to enable him to claim her ripe parted lips with his own.

For a couple of long minutes the champagne glasses on the table at his elbow were ignored as he tasted her with hungry fervour.

Finally, Zia tore her swollen mouth free and lifted a small hand to push back his shoulder in rebuke. 'No… no…no… I know where this heads—only to the bedroom. And then dinner is late and we put the staff out and it's inconsiderate—'

'*Inconsiderate?* Not the word I'd use to describe this particular special evening,' Orazio countered with calm amusement.

His attention was on her hand as he lifted it in his. Beneath her stunned gaze, he slowly slotted a ring onto her engagement finger: an enormous flashing diamond in a setting that reminded her of an opening flower. It was a breathtaking piece of jewellery and light was flooding in from the window beside them, dancing rainbows across the many diamond facets.

Dumbstruck, Zia continued to stare at her hand. 'Er… what? I mean, what is this?'

'You're not that slow on the uptake,' Orazio chided. 'Obviously it's a proposal of marriage. Do I need to get down on one knee to make it seem more real?'

In shock, Zia blinked rapidly, leapt off him as if she had been burned and backed away a few steps on wobbly legs. 'What are you playing at? Is this some kind of a joke?' she exclaimed. 'Please tell me you're not surrendering to all the stupid gossip about us and asking me to marry you to *please* people.'

Raz directed a wickedly appreciative grin at her.

'Where did you get the idea that I'm that easily pushed around by outside forces? I'm as stubborn as a pig and very resistant to doing anything I don't want to do… even as King. It's a role, it's not my *whole* life.'

Zia sucked in a ragged breath to refresh her straining lungs. 'OK,' she said tautly.

She had always believed that there was a little more give in him than he was prepared to concede and she was unsure just how far he would go to grant the population of Mandovia, to whom he was ferociously loyal, what *they* wanted. 'So, why didn't you just ask me to marry you, then? Why sort of sneak a ring on my finger as if I've already said yes?'

Raz sprawled back on the couch with the grace of a prowling tiger and settled brilliant black-lashed green eyes on her pale, tight face. All of a sudden, he acknowledged, nothing was happening as he had dimly assumed it would and he was in a tense scene without a script. Evidently, she had *not* been expecting a marriage proposal from him. That was a huge shock to him.

'I thought you were waiting for me to ask, expecting this to happen,' he remarked ruefully.

Zia shook her head, silky luxurious strands of black hair tumbling round her flushed cheeks. 'No, I wasn't. I assumed we were both simply getting this relationship out of our systems—'

'Like I'd have gone public about us if I'd believed that!' Orazio derided with an edge of annoyance, lifting her glass and extending it to her. 'Bubbly. I warned Harvey—'

'Even your butler knows you were about to propose and I *didn't*?' she condemned.

'If there's a next time I'll be sure to hire one of those planes that skywrites for the proposal!' Raz fielded in a raw undertone. 'Look, seemingly I've got this all wrong, but could you give me an answer?'

'I think you're putting the cart before the horse,' Zia told him in stark, tight syllables. 'I mean, how do you *feel* about me? For me, that's the most important question here. When did you start thinking of me as a possible wife?'

'The first week I met you… I just knew the same moment that you assured me that you didn't want to marry me *either…* That's when I realised that I wasn't as keen to stay single as I had once been. I've become very fond of you, *piccola mia*, and I believe we make an excellent team. You're perfect for me *and* the future reunited Mandovia.'

Fond of her? Zia was fond of her dog, Sausage, but she *loved* Orazio. Struggling to keep her breathing level, the backs of her eyes suddenly prickling with an unwelcome surge of disillusioned tears, she nodded in silence. *Fond, perfect for Mandovia, an excellent team.* A very, *very* practical approach to choosing a future wife and queen. How could she fault him for that? Briefly, she thought of how passionate their nights were and felt that it was a shame that not an ounce of that simmering passion appeared to have been matched by any deeper, more lasting emotion. And that was wounding, but then not everybody got the *whole* fairy tale and the happy-ever-after, she told herself starkly. And certainly to date, she never had.

She was getting the proposal but not the love. Shouldn't she try being grateful for what they did have?

The passion, his kindness, the comfortable lifestyle he was offering her, the status, the goodwill of both their nations? That was plenty, she scolded herself inwardly, and a whole heck of a lot more than she had ever had before.

'I'll take all that into consideration,' she told him in a slightly wobbly undertone as she accepted the glass of champagne and deliberately directed her attention to her spectacular engagement ring. 'Let me sleep on this, Raz. I wasn't expecting you to propose so I need the time to think this over.'

Orazio sat up in a sudden movement that spooked her, all relaxation now openly abandoned. 'What's holding you back?'

Zia winced, wondering how frank she could be without causing lasting offence. 'I appreciate that you think I could be a good partner as a queen and, obviously, we're a popular pairing, so I understand that aspect too. But when it comes to a husband, I'm looking for a bit more—'

'How *much* more?' he demanded, leaning forward, apprehension filling his glittering green eyes, tightening his facial muscles.

'You said you were fond of me, which is rather impersonal. I'm fond of my dog,' she pointed out as she eased the gorgeous diamond off her finger again and gently settled it back down on the coffee table. 'I would prefer a husband who is a little less lukewarm about his feelings for me in the emotional department. From all I've heard, read and seen, marriage can be challenging. It shouldn't be something you enter without the very strongest reasons. I would want my marriage to last and, to be honest, you don't sound sufficiently committed or keen enough on me. I do appreciate that I'm the convenient choice because of who I am and my positive approval rating with our people. But I truly believe that I need to mean *more* than that to you for any marriage between us to succeed. I can't marry you, Raz.'

And with that measured declaration, Zia set her untouched champagne down beside the ring and walked out of the room, Sausage surging up to run at her heels as she headed for her suite in the Queen's Tower.

Well, she had been honest with him, she conceded ruefully, without getting down to the embarrassing nitty-gritty details and telling him bluntly that she wanted love, not fondness. After all, what would be the point in telling him such a thing? A person didn't love to order. A person didn't fall in love with you simply because you loved them. Either he loved you or he didn't and not all the wishing in the world could change that fact.

Yet, inside her, her heart had just cracked right down the middle. She had turned him down even though she loved him, but she needed more from him than fondness, for goodness' sake. Yet the thought of losing Orazio bowed her shoulders and twisted her tummy with pain, sending a chill down her rigid spine. And obviously she would lose him now that she had refused to marry him, she conceded wretchedly.

Before she could settle into her room and the emotional turmoil that was beginning to engulf her, she was informed that she had a visitor. Nobody could have been more surprised than she was to be shown downstairs into one of the formal meeting rooms to find Massimo Caccia waiting for her.

'Massimo?' she said uncertainly.

The older man looked tense and somehow aged since their last meeting, his plump features thinned, dark purple bruises below his eyes. 'Yes, I'm here to make a formal apology,' he told her tautly.

'A formal apology?' Zia repeated uneasily. 'But what for?'

'Please sit down, Your Highness,' he urged anxiously. 'I have a confession to make. I arranged your supposed theft to ensure your return to Mandovia.'

Unpleasant surprise shivered through Zia and she braced a hand on the meeting table beside her, shaken that Orazio's cynical suspicions had been proven correct. 'You *arranged* it?'

And she sank down in the nearest seat in sheer astonishment as Massimo admitted to bribing Sofia Marone's maid to plant her diamond brooch in the cleaning trolley. 'But why?' she queried in disbelief.

'For Mandovia,' he declared uncomfortably. 'Your Highness, have you no idea even *now* how important a symbol you are to the people of Upper Mandovia? I'm just one of those people. I went into the army here in Lower Mandovia but my goal was always to be of use to *our* country—to bring us *all* together.' His hands moved to illustrate his point while he regarded her with deep expectation and a degree of awe that embarrassed her. 'And you can do that. In fact, you *have* done it and though the government does not agree with *what* I did or my methods…it's worked out, hasn't it? I brought you and His Majesty together…'

Zia was too disconcerted by his admission that the theft in London had been orchestrated to entrap her to immediately respond. Obviously, Orazio had suspected that, but she had not really processed the suspicion because she had trustingly believed that it was impossible for a government figure to behave in such a manner. Now she was struggling to accept the reality and Massimo's confession without attacking him. Massimo, who had been so supportive and understanding of her situation in London? Massimo, whom she had innocently trusted because he had seemed to be on her side? My goodness, she was naïve, ridiculously naïve in comparison to Orazio, who had smelt a rat the minute he'd heard her story!

'And what's happening now?' she almost whispered.

'I've been dismissed. The cabinet says my moral outlook is very much wrong and out of step with everyone else's,' Massimo admitted heavily. 'They were very shocked by my actions, none of which were condoned by the government. Even though the end result was exactly what they longed for—our Princess back in Mandovia—my methods were viewed as unacceptable and I'm now the bad guy—'

'Yes,' Zia registered with sudden comprehension. 'But also, in a sense, you *rescued* me, Massimo. Orazio wouldn't want me to admit that, but I won't deny it. Sandrine Beccari had Alina and me trapped. The way you went about the rescue was *wrong*—no denying that—but I can forgive you because, no matter what happens here, it's still better than my life was in London.'

'That is a very generous admission,' Massimo opined in unashamed wonder.

'Not at all. I know what it's like to suffer and get nowhere because people won't listen to you…or because they have no respect for your opinions,' she confided. 'What will you do now?'

'I have been tasked with setting up our first embassy in Japan,' Massimo told her in an undertone. 'I am fortunate indeed to still have employment.'

Ignoring the reality that Massimo was not happy to be exiled to the other side of the world, Zia managed a comforting smile, because if the government could not accept his behaviour, he was better still employed than out of work. 'And you'll be in your element,' she forecast with confidence. 'You'll get it moving fast. You're an action guy.'

'Thank you, Your Highness,' Massimo murmured with deep feeling, his dark brown eyes glistening with appreciation. 'I don't deserve your good wishes but I do appreciate them. You're a forgiving person…perhaps it is good that you are paired with the King, who is *not*, at all, a forgiving person.'

'Orazio could surprise you,' Zia almost whispered.

But that was that. Massimo departed after wishing her all the best for the future, visibly looking forward to the event of a royal wedding. She would not have dared to admit that she had just turned down the King's proposal. And she was still wondering if she had done the right thing. Had she made the right decision?

All or nothing?

She went back upstairs for a belated dinner although goodness knew she had no appetite. Braced to face Orazio again, she was disconcerted when he failed to join her in the dining room. Of course, he would scarcely be in the mood to want to share a table with her, she conceded reluctantly. He had asked her to marry him in the clumsiest way, as if the very reality that they were currently sharing a bed was a sufficient reason for him to assume that she would agree.

But then, if he was speaking the truth in saying that he had always *expected* to marry her, it meant that from the outset of their affair they had both misunderstood each other's intentions. Was that her fault? Or his? Had he genuinely always had the view that they would end up together? Was she guilty of being blind and cynical? She had always assumed that he would get bored with her and would want to move on. But what were they going to do now when everything had fallen apart?

Her heart sank as she got ready for bed. Well, that was the state of play, only it wasn't play, she thought heavily. It was her heart in the balance. Orazio had done what everybody expected him to do. His people wanted him to marry her, to make her his Queen. Where was the choice there for him when they were already living together? He had taken the next step, the *anticipated* next step. Could she fault him for that proposal that had not been a proposal at all and had, instead, been more of an assumption?

He was *still* the guy she loved, she reflected unhappily. Perhaps she was expecting too much from him? She had disappointed him. He had wanted to marry her. It might be that he wanted to marry her for the wrong reasons but that wouldn't diminish his sense of failure. He had seemed to believe that she was waiting for his proposal. In other words, he had believed that she was expecting it and might have acted differently had he known otherwise.

An extraordinary shard of compassion shivered through her then. Orazio was always so determined to be cool. It was almost a character trait. He'd seen it all, done it all and he didn't get down and dirty in the way other people did, she acknowledged. His true feelings were kept private and he kept them to himself as though his life depended on it. Maybe that severe reserve had served him well as an unloved child, as a reluctant monarch where personal feelings weren't welcome. Her heart squeezed at that realisation as she recalled his mother's unemotional greeting, an attack on his apparent choices rather than a loving maternal embrace and a family reunion.

In a sudden movement, she clambered out of bed again, snatched up a robe in the dressing room and set off for Orazio's room. Even though he was probably angry with her, it felt wrong to her that they should be apart after such a rupture between them. She raised a brow when she thought of the adjoining principal bedrooms at the country house where they had spent several very happy and relaxed weekends together. In the royal castle, heading to Orazio's bedroom meant traversing three corridors, two stone staircases and then mounting the many steps to the King's Tower. No greater sign of his parents' unhappy marriage could have been found than the sheer distance between their respective bedrooms.

She didn't knock because she wasn't sure that he was even in his room. Simply walking in, she stilled when she saw him sprawled across the rumpled bed, sitting up with his back braced against the carved headboard. His shirt hung open on his bronzed, muscular torso and he was still wearing his jeans.

'I blew the proposal…' Raz said with a bitter edge as he studied her.

'Yes,' Zia conceded in the smouldering silence. 'It was a car crash because I wasn't prepared for it and you simply assumed that I would agree—'

'And then I said all the wrong things,' Raz contributed with a frustrated wave of an eloquent lean brown hand. 'And even as I voiced them, I knew it was the wrong stuff, but I'm very wary about sharing private feelings.' And then, in an abrupt movement, he sat up and vaulted off the bed, long powerful legs settling onto solid ground again. 'No, that's a lie. I could've told you the truth but I didn't want to expose myself to that extent—'

'Why not?' she interrupted.

Orazio sucked in oxygen and his broad chest expanded. 'I haven't told a woman that I loved her since my mother laughed in my face and told me I'd soon grow out of thinking that I loved her. And, you know, she was right. In the end, you *do* stop loving people who don't love you back.'

'I'm sorry she said that to you,' Zia whispered in a pained undertone. 'I'm sorry that you grew up with that.'

'I was only six years old. She told me that because she was a queen she *had* to give birth to a child who could be the heir to the throne and that I was that child. Conceived out of necessity alone. I still recall returning to my room and trying to figure out the spelling of necessity to look it up in the dictionary.'

'Oh, Raz…' Releasing her breath in a pained sigh, Zia crossed the depth of rich Persian rug beneath her feet and closed her arms round him as he stood there looking grim, with his expressive green eyes awash with sorrow from that old wound. He was rigid in her hold, every muscle tightly clenched with tension. 'Don't even think about it any more,' she urged, soft fingers stretching up to soothingly caress his long, lean back. 'I'm different. *We're* different. That's not our story.'

'But you still don't want to marry me,' Orazio bit out rawly.

'Because I need *more* than fondness,' she muttered fiercely.

Orazio clenched his even white teeth and bit out a curse. 'How can you be so blind? I loved you before I even understood what love for a woman *was*. I loved you virtually from the beginning because I would never have plunged us into a sexual relationship *without* that connection. We were always meant to be. To be something *more*, to be a true couple in love…and that was absolutely my dream. Not to marry for the sake of it, for having a queen or children or any of that…to have a woman whom I loved and who might love me back, something real and lasting and for ever—'

'You want what I want,' she exclaimed in shocked appreciation at what she hadn't grasped and what he had always intended. 'And I love you too…*so much*.'

Orazio froze and then just as suddenly relaxed as he tasted her heartfelt words and luxuriated in them. He drew her fully into his arms, still stunned by her whispered admission. 'You love me? Then *why*—?'

'I turned down the proposal because I thought you didn't love me,' she confided in a rush. 'I couldn't agree to marry you *without* love—'

'But I *do* love you—'

'Only you didn't tell me that,' she pointed out helplessly.

'So, I totally messed up?'

'Yes,' Zia sighed. 'You didn't give me a proposal that any woman would want.'

Orazio threw back his shoulders and breathed in deep and long at that statement. 'So, I need to do it again the *right* way—'

'No, no…that would be overkill,' Zia objected afresh, shaking her hand in front of his face, wanting the weight of her ring back on it. 'Where's my ring gone?'

'You took it off. You didn't want it—'

'If I had known that you loved me, it would never have come off my finger again,' she admitted ruefully.

A sudden grin illuminated Orazio's lean bronzed features. He freed her and strode across the room to retrieve the small item from a dresser. As she hovered, he returned and grasped her hand to show her the ring that she had rejected. *'So?'*

'Yes, I want to marry you. Yes, I love you and want us to be together,' she murmured feverishly and he slid the ring back onto her finger.

'I do *truly* love you,' he breathed, green eyes glowing with intensity, and a little quiver ran through her, starting in her tummy to flutter like butterflies before sliding up to make her heart race and then down into her pelvis where it lit up her body in a sensual response.

'And I love you so much,' she confessed, half under her breath.

'I felt sick at the very idea of losing you. I couldn't bear that,' Orazio admitted in a raw undertone. 'You're everything I ever wanted in a woman…and you appeared before I even *knew* what I wanted,' he explained remorsefully. 'And then suddenly there you were, the whole package I didn't believe I could ever find and a true partner.'

Her hands, the diamond glittering on her slender finger even in the shadowy room, smoothed slowly up over his lean torso in an appreciative surge. 'It never occurred to me that you could be serious about me.'

'Really? You didn't think I'd know a good thing when I found it?' he scoffed. 'You're beautiful and sexy, charming, loyal and truthful, friendly, unspoiled, caring. You're everything I didn't even know I was dreaming of in my future wife. I would've been a very stupid guy if I hadn't realised what a catch you were, but you were like quicksilver in my fingers…always on the brink of running away if I seemed to be too serious or I seemed to want too much from you—'

'I was scared of getting serious with anyone—'

'Therefore when you said stuff about us being casual, I listened and I couldn't argue because I didn't want to risk frightening you off. You were so stubborn and independent. I didn't want you to worry that I was one of those men who try to clip a woman's wings or restrict her, so I had to back off and not say the things I wanted to and tie strings to you. But I didn't want just strings attached, I wanted freaking chains!' he gritted in a driven admission, welding her to every line of his lean, hard body with possessive hands. 'I've learned a lot about myself since I met you.'

'What did you learn?'

'That I'm possessive and territorial and jealous when it comes to the woman I love. Every time Giancarlo Marone oiled up to you, I wanted to plant a fist in his smirking face and tell him to back off! But you hadn't given me that right…' he completed gruffly. 'Have I got the right now?'

Hugging her new awareness of his strong feelings for her, Zia was able to laugh for the first time that evening. 'I should think the ring will warn him that I'm a lost cause and a waste of his time now,' she contended. 'When do you think we'll get married?'

'As soon as it can be arranged,' Orazio declared, lifting her slight body up against him and dropping a hungry kiss on her lush lips as she wriggled responsively against him. 'I want you tied to me by every device available because I'm terrified of you changing your mind and deciding you can do better than me.'

'I'm not about to do that,' she told him warmly. 'But from now on, we talk about feelings even though you don't like doing it, so that we don't get crossed wires between us again.'

He came down over her, brilliant eyes dancing with amusement as he got caught up in her voluminous silky robe before he could strip it off and discard it. 'There is a small, very sexy, curvy body under here somewhere,' he teased as he came up against an equally flowy and flouncy nightie. 'It's just a matter of finding it.'

Zia pushed at his shoulder until he leant back from her and she sat up, whipped off her last garment and lay back against the pillows, grinning up at him as his heated gaze roamed over her bare, bountiful curves. 'Now do your worst.'

'My very best, *piccola mia*,' he contradicted huskily, looping her hair back to trace a fevered path down the length of her slender neck to her delicate collarbone, making her shiver with intense awareness. 'I love you more than I ever loved anyone or anything in my life and I can't believe that you're finally mine.'

'And I can't believe that you're mine,' she whispered, hauling him down to her with eager hands as his own hands roved over every sensitive curve he could reach and the wicked hum of desire began to rise inside her like a tide. 'I love you.'

He was hers, she thought thankfully, utterly unaccustomed to the warmth of happiness flooding through her. Nobody had ever made her feel so important, so precious or so necessary. Afloat on those joyous new feelings, anchored by that overpowering conviction that she was finally home and safe, Zia gave herself up to the passion and the sheer delight of being with the male she loved.

EPILOGUE

On their wedding anniversary, Zia glanced at the official portrait on the wall of her in the wedding gown she had worn almost four years ago. Orazio had insisted that that image remain on display in the drawing room…as if she would ever forget that day, a public holiday for Mandovia. No, she would never forget that special day or her wonderful embroidered handmade lace dress, emblazoned with all the symbols cherished by their people from the wild flowers to their most treasured birds. She still adored the dainty pearl-studded satin shoes she had worn that were as comfortable as slippers. They had spent the weeks of their honeymoon on the yacht cruising the Mediterranean.

Changes had come thick and fast after their wedding, for the reunification had taken place within months and elections in both countries had taken place immediately to allow for the choice of a more representative integrated government. Upper Mandovia was so unspoilt that it was doing very well in the tourist trade with walkers and nature lovers. Hotels and hostels were slowly being built, along with more modern schools and medical facilities. The boom in construction had ensured that unemployment figures were falling fast.

Zia had conceived their first child soon after the wedding and, after a fairly trouble-free pregnancy, Luca had been born with a shock of her black hair and his father's green eyes. Now a toddler, Luca was lively, inquisitive and loving. His little sister had arrived the previous year. Bianca Alina was as blonde as Orazio had been as a child with her mother's dark blue eyes. She was a pretty, quite demanding baby, who screamed at anything she didn't like, whether it be a bath or a sudden noise that disturbed her peace. Her father swore that she had her mother's stubborn, suspicious nature but Zia was convinced that Bianca was getting a little spoiled by the amount of attention she received from her parents, the castle staff and the nannies in the royal nursery.

She frowned as Luca darted in to scoop up one of Bianca's toys and his sister loosed a warning shout of temper. As she retrieved it from her laughing son, who simply loved to tease his baby sibling, she scolded him. Her retreated with a wicked grin that was the very image of his father's while two small dogs capered around their feet, hoping for some further excitement.

Sausage had acquired a sidekick when Zia had stumbled on a female mini dachshund in a shelter and in need of a home. She had called her Egg because she had a little domed head that suggested her family tree might be rather more mixed than Sausage's pedigreed heritage. The two were now so close that they shared a basket, although Egg was definitely the boss and neither of them were as well trained as Raz's mastiffs in spite of his efforts in that direction.

Two years earlier, Sandrine had received a prison sentence for forging Zia's signature and defrauding her charge of her inheritance. Of course, the cash she had frittered away would never be recovered but Zia was satisfied that her former guardian had been punished and the house in London, which she had no happy memories of living in, had been sold soon afterwards. She tried not to look back too often to the darker parts of her past, preferring to look forward to her much more promising future.

Alina, in the meantime, had settled happily into her sister's home in the village where both elderly ladies had grown up and Zia visited them when she was in the area, particularly when she had the children with her. Raz and she still spent occasional weekends at the country house, which they had renovated from roof to basement. It was quiet and peaceful there and sometimes exactly what they needed after a particularly busy week.

Now, as she heard her son whoop and race across the room, she stood up, smoothing down her elegant short silvery blue dress, a warm smile tilting her lips. Luca raced into Orazio's arms to be swept up into a hug. Bianca noticed her father and began to crawl laboriously towards him while letting out a little squeak of complaint at being expected to make that much effort.

Raz set down Luca and scooped up a beaming Bianca as their nannies arrived to take over for the evening. It was their wedding anniversary, after all, and instead of settling for a fancy meal at the castle they were heading to Paris for the night. 'You look fantastic, *piccola mia*. I want to eat you alive,' he whispered thickly as he bent down by her ear.

'But you have to wait until we're airborne,' she reminded him, knowing that if she accompanied him to their bedroom for him to change, he would drag her into bed and make them late for their flight.

They didn't have his and her bedrooms any longer. They had knocked rooms together to make one large room they could share and which could accommodate separate dressing rooms. It meant that the children were closer to them at night as well.

'Can't wait that long,' Orazio told her with deadly seriousness. 'I'll shower on the plane. Let's leave now.'

'So, tell me about your very long day with the politicians,' she suggested once they were in the limousine on the way to the airport.

'They're thinking of inviting Massimo Caccia back before the elections. Apparently he's done a fabulous job in Japan and at record speed. They value his cunning. He gets the job done.'

'Yes, he does,' she agreed, running a small hand down over one powerful thigh. 'Would you mind? I know you don't like him.'

'There are two sides to every coin, *piccola mia*. He freed you from that ghastly Beccari woman and gave me a chance with you,' he murmured, his breathing fracturing beneath her caressing touch. 'In all honesty, I couldn't dislike anyone who can work a miracle of that nature.'

Glittering green eyes encountered hers and he stretched over and kissed her breathless. 'Did I ever tell you what a little witch you can be?'

'You might have mentioned it once or twice,' she gasped, wanting more, wanting him with the sudden seething hunger that just engulfed her sometimes, but knowing that they had to wait until they were on the plane and finally alone.

On their private jet, she reclined back on the bed in their cabin like a temptress, wearing the superb diamond necklace he had given her for their anniversary. Teamed with the magnificent diamonds she already owned, she glittered like a window display and he couldn't take his eyes off her as he stood by the side of the bed, dropped his towel and came over her, all male, very aroused.

'I love you more today than I loved you on the day I married you,' he intoned in a roughened voice. 'And that's really saying something. The longer I'm with you, the more I need you...'

'I love you too,' she whispered happily as the passion flamed into a smouldering fever that worked up quite an appetite for their fancy meal in Paris.

* * * * *

Did King's Promised Princess *leave you wanting more? Then you're certain to love these other sparkling stories from Lynne Graham!*

Greek's One-Night Babies
His Royal Bride Replacement
Shock Greek Heir
Unveiling the Wrong Bride
Her Two Greek Secrets

Available now!

If you loved King's Promised Princess*,*
why not try Lynne Graham's last romance,
Her Two Greek Secrets*!*

CHAPTER ONE

Aristide Romanos, billionaire entrepreneur, was relieved when his senior PA, Georgio, contrived to give him a slight smile from his hospital bed. 'Only one more scan to go and I'll be free to leave, sir.'

Aristide winced. He wasn't always the most considerate employer but even he was not about to drag an employee with a broken ankle straight out of hospital. 'No, you won't be. You'll stay here until a medic tells you to leave and then only to return to the hotel where you will rest.'

A car crash in the airport car park had taken out Aristide's entire personal team of six. Three were down with concussion, one with a broken arm and another with a mix of injuries. Currently, Georgio was the only member of his staff to remain in full possession of his wits.

'But, sir…what will you—?'

'I will proceed to Traxis.' Aristide paused to enjoy Georgio's look of disbelief. 'I *can* work alone. I will do a tour and meet senior personnel. Another team will arrive to assist me tomorrow. Relax, Georgio, you're on sick leave.'

Aristide knew that his PA didn't find it any easier to

relax than he did. Georgio, like Aristide, was a driven type-A personality. Ignoring the attention that his six-foot-four-inch, well-built frame and sleek, dark good looks garnered from the female staff, he strode out of the private hospital and back into his limo, directing his driver to his destination. Another takeover, another day, he reflected wryly, but, undeniably, work was the spice of life to him.

He scanned a text from a former lover and without hesitation asked her to lose his number. He was only twenty-eight but he didn't do repeats with women, never had, never would. Sex was just sex, a necessity for a male of his appetites, but it could still be controlled within certain boundaries. An entire weekend was as close as Aristide got to commitment. He was a shameless playboy, fashioned that way from growing up with a father who couldn't resist women. Ex-wives, ex-partners and discarded lovers and children had littered his father's life.

That kind of background left scars that Aristide was fully aware of having. But, even so, he simply didn't want female drama in his life: no broken hearts, no accusations of infidelity, no jealous scenes, no betrayals, no lies. Aristide could not imagine having only *one* woman in his life and he was even less keen on the option of ever fathering a child of his own. Without a doubt, his last will and testament would spread his wealth across the best of his many relatives.

One month later

Tabby checked the test and imagined her eyes shooting out wide on stalks like a cartoon character telegraphing fear and alarm. Her blood ran cold in her veins, shock rippling through her. She was *pregnant*. She sucked in a deep breath to ward off the dizziness assailing her. How on earth could she have been so stupid? So reckless? She, who prided herself on her intelligence and self-discipline, had just utterly messed up her life *and* her poor sister's. At the eleventh hour, she would have to back out of the business marriage she had contracted to complete and her twin, Violet, would have to take her place.

And that was only the *first* of the mistakes she had made, she acknowledged wretchedly. She had messed up so badly that she was horribly ashamed of herself. Furthermore, now she would have a child to raise alone, a baby who would be totally dependent on her currently useless self!

How on earth had she contrived to sink so low, so fast?

And the memories began to flutter back in a series of episodes like some ghastly soap opera…

It had started with their mother Lucia's illness, persistent cancer, which had dogged her for many years and right then their beloved mum had been at her last post. Her sole hope for survival was a new experimental drug on a clinical trial in the USA. But it cost money to get a place on such trials and one thing Lucia and her two daughters had never had was surplus cash.

Indeed the only wealthy person they even knew, and they scarcely *knew* him, was their grandfather, Tomaso Barone, he of the hard heart who had cast off their mother when she was a teenager who chose to marry the wrong man. And regrettably, Sam Blessington, their father, had been very much the wrong man, a feckless artist with a taste for booze, violence and other women and no interest at all in his twin daughters. Throughout their childhood there had been sobering experiences like bailiffs, homelessness and hunger and, on several occasions, Lucia had begged her father to help them. But not *once* had he come through for his estranged only child. So, when Violet and Tabby had made an appointment to meet Tomaso and ask for his financial assistance to enable their mother to get on that trial, they had not been optimistic.

It had been a huge shock when Tomaso had looked across his giant office desk and said, 'Yes, I will help your mother *this* time…if in turn one of you does something for me.'

'Anything!' she and Violet had promised simultaneously with no idea whatsoever of what he had been about to propose: a marriage with the heir to his rival competitor's company to cement a business deal.

'As your sister has a child, it will obviously be you, Viola, who takes up this wonderful opportunity,' her grandfather had insisted. He wasn't even aware that she was called Tabitha because her drunken father had bungled registering their birth names. On paper she was Viola Tabitha but in actuality she had always gone by her middle name.

Of course, there had been no choice but to agree, not when he had been dangling the bait of that all-important cash for their mother's benefit. The very belief that his grandchild would get to wed the super-rich heir to Renzetti Pharmaceuticals and carry on what he somehow deemed to be *his* legacy had delighted the older man. Neither Violet nor Tabitha had guessed that, when it came to actually handing over the money, he would welch on the deal with the excuse that they had to wait longer for it.

Only they hadn't *had* time to wait when their mother was so frail and instead Tabby had had to ask her future husband's lawyers for the sum as conditional on her signing the pre-nup before the wedding. And in return, she had been asked to reduce the five-year marital term to three instead and of course she had agreed, not wanting to have her own life derailed for any longer than necessary.

Consenting to marry a male who couldn't even be bothered to meet her prior to the wedding had freaked Tabby out. It had felt as though every one of her personal choices was being stolen from her: she was to marry a stranger and live in his home and put up with whatever he chose to throw at her for three long endless years. A prison camp had sounded more appealing than that, especially after she had read the clause relating to her personal behaviour, which barred her from meeting any men or consorting with them in any way.

Why? Tabby had never had a man in her life or particularly *wanted* one. Her father had for ever soured her on the male sex but, even so, she still hadn't liked being a virgin at almost twenty-two. She'd seen that as a rite of passage into adulthood that she hadn't wished to wait another three years to experience. A mere physical thing, a bodily thing, and not something to make a big deal about, she had decided, in her innocence.

And that decision, Tabby recognised, and that rash attitude had brought her to her current crisis of having conceived an unplanned child. It should have been something she could celebrate and she blamed *him* for the fact she couldn't because *he* had already accused *her* of trying to set him up when the condom failed. What kind of madness had possessed her when she'd thought that she could have a simple one-night stand as other women did? Well, for her, it had gone badly wrong and she blamed inexperience and her ignorance in bedding such a dreadful choice of a guy for the consequences.

Certainly, the day it had happened, she had had no idea of what lay ahead. It had begun as a normal shift in her office temp job in a large insurance company where she worked for Ed Stokes, a harmlessly inefficient middle manager, who was, nonetheless, related to the CEO, who absolutely never showed his face in the building.

'Julian…' aka, the CEO of Traxis '…suggested that I look after this senior audit chap coming in,' Ed had explained. 'But I want you to do it instead because you have a degree in accounting and I work in sales.'

There had been no point reminding Ed that Tabby hated accounting and had learned that any day she preferred general office admin to perusing profit and loss figures. Ed was the boss and she had an easy job as long as she took care of all the many things that intimidated mild-mannered, socially awkward Ed, like meeting new people or dealing with senior staff. He shunted off everything he disliked onto Tabby and he got away with it too because he was on first-name terms with the big boss.

Tabby had hung about Reception awaiting the arrival of the VIP accountant with nothing but the name of the company he worked for in terms of information: Millwright and Sons.

A very tall, commanding male with a shock of cropped black curls had entered and the receptionist had greeted him while Tabby had hovered uncertainly by her side, sheltering behind the desk the more she noticed about the new arrival. The fabulous custom fit of his black suit, the unusual formality of the silk tie and closed collar on his shirt, the reality that he was so tall she had to crane her neck and tip her head back even to steal a look at his lean, bronzed face.

'Mr Millwright?' the receptionist asked hesitantly.

The reference to his London audit team, who wouldn't be arriving until the next day, relaxed Aristide into the belief that he was expected.

'No, I'm Aristide Romanos,' he announced.

'I'm Tabitha Blessington, Mr Romanos…' another voice interposed and he turned his proud dark head to look at her. 'My boss asked that I show you around.'

Aristide was taken aback that the CEO was not in place to greet him but, as a male, he was immediately captured by the angelic fairness of the speaker. Aristide liked blondes, he always had, but rarely had he met one quite so beautiful, who had not plundered every cosmetic trick in the box. This one had flawless translucent skin like fine china and not even a trace of lipstick on her sensually plump lips. Not to mention huge blue eyes, perfect features and a mane of pale blonde hair that looked as natural as a child's. She had an unspoilt look new to his experience and it grabbed his interest, which would at best be…fleeting, he assumed without a doubt of that in his handsome head. An arrogance taught by countless very willing ladies in his past.

He didn't view her as an employee. He owned dozens

of companies. He took them over and sorted out their issues before installing trusted executives. He might well never visit Traxis Insurance again, so he didn't consider himself bound by any rules of the workplace.

'Miss Blessington,' Aristide returned as she extended a slender hand to his much bigger paw, the size differential between them making his shapely mouth quirk with amusement. She was small and unexpectedly slight with fewer curves than was usually his preference but his interest abated not a jot.

'Tabitha…or, er… Tabby will do,' she heard herself say like a woman in a dream because he was truly the most gorgeous male she had ever met and she felt overwhelmed by his presence. As if that were not bad enough, a sensation like an electric shock tremored down her arm as their fingers barely brushed. Static electricity, she gathered, but that unnerved her even more. Her hand retreated, fingers curling back in on themselves to drop to her side.

'Where would you like to start, Mr Romanos?' she asked shakily, refusing to look back up at him again, eager to get moving, to do anything other than be forced to concentrate her eyes on him a second time.

First off, she had collided with dark eyes as impenetrable as black glass and then he had tipped his strong jaw a little as she looked and those eyes had flashed to glittering gold in the sunlight. After that, brain power had kind of receded while he stood there, perfectly at ease and assured, and simply studied her in brooding silence from beneath straight ebony brows and lush black thick lashes. She had worried that she had greeted him wrong or somehow done something he took amiss and nervous tension had almost eaten her alive

'Top floor…obviously,' Aristide told her somewhat drily as he took the lead in heading for the lift, punching the button with an impatient air. 'Tell me about yourself…'

'I'm a temp,' Tabby admitted, hoping that any mistakes she made would be excused on that basis because this male struck her as unlike any accountant she had ever met and she had met a lot while studying and training. 'I work as a PA for Mr Stokes in the sales department—'

'Why am I being welcomed by a temp?' Aristide enquired, watching a flush of colour wash her dainty cheekbones, wondering if she coloured up like that as she came and wholly resolved to find out. It was an instant attraction, he reckoned, an attraction stronger than anything he had felt in quite a few years. He didn't want to recall the last occasion it had happened to him and he blocked off the recollection fast, determined not to revisit that time when he had been young and trusting and really pretty naïve about women and how manipulative they could be when the prize was big enough.

'I don't know, Mr Romanos. I was just asked to come down here. I think it was a request from our CEO—'

'And what's he like?'

'I've never met him,' she said honestly. 'But I think he goes on holiday a lot because he sends photos to my boss…you know the sort of thing. Skiing in the Alps, deep sea diving in the Caribbean, so I assume he's one of those men's men, who like to get physical.'

'As do we all,' Aristide purred, thinking that she

could be a mine of information even if it was only common gossip. 'How long have you worked here?'

'Six months. My contract keeps getting renewed, probably because my boss likes me—'

An ebony brow hitched. '*Likes* you?'

Tabby went pink. 'Oh, not like *that*, for goodness' sake! He's a married man with a load of young kids—'

'That doesn't stop a lot of men from straying,' Aristide said with cynical bite. 'My own father was never happier than when he was playing away…'

'Mine too,' Tabby muttered helplessly, quite unsure as to why they should be discussing such things when they had only just met but encouraged by his confidence into giving her own.

Aristide clamped his lips closed, unnerved by how personal he had got with her. He never verged on spilling secrets with his lovers and remained a closed book to all of them. That was a very deliberate policy. He didn't create common ground, he didn't *relax*. But there was something about Tabby, something uniquely warm and inviting and, curiously, she had caught him off guard for a moment.

'Where is everybody?' he asked as they stepped out onto the top floor where he had expected to find the senior staff assembled for his arrival.

'Give me the name of whoever you wish to speak to and I will get him or her for you. Our finance director is on the floor below,' she told him expectantly.

Aristide had nothing to say to a finance director who hadn't even made it to the top floor in a business that was failing from lack of vigour and direction. 'You can give me a general tour instead,' he told her. 'While you tell me more about yourself.'

Women loved to talk about themselves and rarely realised how much they were revealing in so doing. He had learned that as a child while carefully navigating the stony pathways and fresh rules laid down by every new woman who entered his home. It was second nature for him to explore a woman's background and goals while remaining on the emotional sidelines. All he had to do was plant the occasional encouraging word and he found out about her mother's fragile health, her sister, Violet's bakery and the child her twin was adopting. Clearly they shared very close family ties and he wondered vaguely what that would be like to experience. He heard about how she had gone to university to study accountancy because that had seemed to offer the best hope of a decent career.

'Only I hated it,' Tabby told him.

'Then, why didn't you change your subject?'

'I had already acquired a student loan debt for that year and I didn't want to add to that by dropping out, so I stuck with it and qualified,' Tabby admitted. 'But I think now that I'm working, I should've changed. That's life, isn't it? You don't have a crystal ball to see into the future—'

'Some day you may have your own business and you'll be glad of it then,' Aristide forecast.

Tabitha blinked, not quite sure she wanted to sign up for her own business as she knew her sister worked unbelievably long hours running the bakery. If that was what it would take, she wasn't sure she was ambitious enough to make that jump to greater responsibility. In time, perhaps, but at not yet twenty-two she had ample years ahead in which to create new goals.

Aristide suggested a view of the office space prepared for him. She took him down to the next floor to the empty office right next to the finance director and bustled off to provide him with refreshments. He had no complaint to make about her attitude but she definitely hadn't grasped who he was, he acknowledged. And in a twisty way he kind of enjoyed that ignorance and liked her for not being flirty and all over him as females generally were in his radius. It was oddly refreshing to see the way she looked at him with that warm smile in her eyes that he had never received from a woman before.

But then, he was like all men, he told himself cynically. She was beautiful and he wanted her. Naturally that had to be affecting his judgement. She was sincere and naturally friendly and Aristide was most definitely not accustomed to receiving purely friendly vibes from a woman. Of course, he had immediately wondered if she already had a man in her life, but he also reckoned, with an inner smile, that he would already have heard about such a man if he existed because Tabby didn't keep much to herself.

She just chattered like a stream wending its difficult way through a complex labyrinth but strangely it didn't irritate him, nor did the sudden conversational jumps. He wasn't used to chat with the women he took to bed. He was usually gone too soon after for such frills. Had he been missing out on something? Was it because she was a few years younger than most of the women he met? What was different about her? That lack of visible vanity? That easy laughter? That soothing silence that fell when he hitched a brow and she paused to see what he wanted from her. She was being professional to a superior, not encouragingly submissive.

Out in the tiny kitchenette, Tabby was brewing coffee and her mind was all over the place as though an avalanche had recently engulfed her… *Aristide.* She was totally convinced that she had found the guy she would accomplish that one-night-stand challenge with. He was so beautiful that she had had to force herself to stop staring at him. Her attraction to him was off-the-scale intense and she had never met with that before. He was considerate and interested in her as a person. Perhaps, best of all, he would just be passing through and she wouldn't see him again once his new team of auditors arrived the following day. He had to work for a very large firm because he had mentioned the accident at the airport and if that firm could muster another six employees that fast, they had to be big and important.

'Mr Roma—' she said, flushed from her current thoughts as she walked back into the office carrying a tray.

'Aristide,' he corrected, disconcerting her. 'Will you have dinner with me tonight?'

Her lower lip parted from the upper and she felt his shrewd dark gaze welding to hers, lifting her chin to say, 'I think I would like that—'

Me too, Aristide was tempted to say, watching the tip of her tongue steal out to moisten her full lip, suddenly rigid with sheer lust to a degree that shook him. With her that reaction was instant and he didn't like anything that felt that uncontrolled grabbing a hold of him. It was always *just* sex for him, never anything more, and maybe it was the dreamy deep blue of her eyes that affected him or the softness of her highly feminine face but he still heard himself murmur the warning, 'It will only be one night…'

And to his total surprise, she gave him a huge smile and nodded. 'Perfect,' she told him, while pouring his black coffee and offering him a selection of biscuits, which he ignored. If only all her sex were so practical, he reasoned, while wondering how on earth she could be wholesome one minute and coolly rational and cynical the next. *Perfect?* Women usually wanted and expected a whole lot more from Aristide than one night. In truth, it stung a little that she appeared so content with that likelihood.

He watched her eat three biscuits in succession while he thought about that oddity. In between times she told him about the pervy employee none of the young women would get into a lift with, the executive PA madly in love with her boss and the security guard with the sick wife at the front, who brought her fresh vegetables from his allotment. She gave no names. Even so, she was… indiscreet but warm and entertaining, he decided with a generosity that would have astounded his hospitalised team because he had never tolerated gossip and lighter moments during his working day.

At noon, having seen even the basement service level of the building, Aristide informed Tabby that he had a meeting elsewhere and took his leave of her in the foyer. 'If you give me your address I'll pick you up tonight at eight,' he murmured lightly.

And she did, stumbling a little over the syllables, far more excited by the idea of a date than she felt she ought to be. After all, no one knew better than her how untrustworthy men could be. Of course, she had met exceptions to that rule, hadn't allowed her father's cruelties to turn her into a man-hater. She did have occasional dates, although none had amounted to much because she had never been attracted enough to get closer to a guy or to take that risk on catching feelings that weren't even wanted.

But the knowledge that she was to marry a stranger in six weeks and do without socialising or having sex if *she* wanted sex was a restriction her pride and self-respect could not accept. This night with Aristide would be *her* choice, her chance to assert her rights over her own body while she still could. There was no way she was running the risk that her stranger husband might be expecting bed privileges into the bargain and that he would then become her *first* lover. No, that little detail would be taken care of off stage and prior to that stupid marriage when nobody would even know about it.

And then, if her mother required some very expensive further treatment to continue her life, as the wife of the wealthy Tore Renzetti, she would be easily able to afford to cover the costs. Why else would she continue agreeing to the marriage after their grandfather had virtually refused to pay up for his daughter's care? With the number of health crises their mother had suffered in recent years, Tabby knew that she had to be aware of the risk that more might lie ahead.

Tabby adored her mother, even if she hadn't always been a mother she could respect as a woman. Lucia Blessington was a very caring, compassionate person and endlessly supportive of her twin girls. Even though her daughters had had a very unhappy childhood while their father was still around, Tabby and Violet had forgiven Lucia for giving their horrible father too many chances to reform.

Now that their parents were divorced and they had no further contact with Sam Blessington, their lives had become calm and peaceful. Now there was no man coming home in a drunken rage and lashing out with his fists or frittering away their mother's earnings. Now Violet and Tabby between them could look forward to keeping their mother out of those low-paid jobs that had been all she was able to get while they were still children.

'Julian's flying back early from his break in Cuba,' Ed informed Tabby worriedly when she returned after lunch. 'He told me that Traxis has been taken over. We'll just have to hope that it's not to one of those asset-strippers, keen to throw us all out of work and sell the building!'

Tabby got back to the flat she shared with several other girls that evening and went straight to her room to trail out her wardrobe and decide what to wear. But it wasn't *really* a date, she reminded herself. He had been quite clear about what it would be and she was fine with that, wasn't she?

The stirring of unease within her warned her that she was less confident than she would have liked about her decision. After all, here she was heading for twenty-two years of age and no *right* male had come along. She hadn't fallen in love and contrived to share a bed in the more natural way. She hadn't even been insanely attracted to a guy until that very same day. So, Aristide was simply the best available option. That was all the evening would be.

It would be like a date, Aristide was thinking with a frown while he showered. And he didn't *do* dates. What was it about Tabitha Blessington that knocked him off balance? As a rule, he met women at events, in businesses or through friends. He didn't ask them out anyplace, he just took them home, whether that be to a hotel or one of his properties. Dinner engagements didn't enter the proceedings. But he had had the suspicion that she would say no if he framed his desire any more frankly. And he hadn't wanted that. No, he hadn't wanted that at all. *Thee mou*, when had he last been this worked up about being with a woman? It was nonsensical and out of character.

By the time the door buzzer went, Tabby was dressed and ready, clad in a casual blue mini dress and a pair of high heels. She hadn't bothered with make-up. After all, it wasn't some romantic date, she reminded herself, opening the door to a middle-aged stranger.

'Mr Romanos is waiting in the car for you, Miss Blessington.'

Romanos, *that* was his name. She hadn't quite caught it when she'd first met him and then hadn't liked to ask him to repeat it lest he think she was pretty incompetent. 'And you are?' she queried quietly.

'His driver…'

Tabby followed the older man down the stairs, her brow furrowed. His *driver*? Who had a driver in London where most travelled by public transport? Only very well-off people. Possibly he was a director in the accountancy firm, she reasoned uncertainly.

She was extremely rattled to find the door of a silver limousine falling open for her arrival. Aristide folded out to his full height and gave her a slashing smile. In that moment, he looked so heart-stoppingly handsome and charismatic that her mouth ran dry and her wits might as well have been dandelion clocks floating in the breeze.

'You look amazing,' he murmured huskily, ushering her into the limo while his driver hovered, openly disconcerted by his employer's presence on the pavement.

No regrets about making the dinner date, Aristide was already thinking as he sank in beside her. The blue of her eyes matched the dress or maybe the blue of the dress heightened the colour of her eyes. He blinked, wondering why he was abstracted enough to think such a thing while simultaneously acknowledging that she was even more beautiful than he remembered her being only hours earlier, pale hair like rumpled silk lying across her narrow shoulders, a heart-shaped silver locket at her delicate collarbone. Somehow his brain conjured up an image of sapphires there instead.

'So, it seems that I've misunderstood who you are somewhere along the way,' Tabby remarked stiffly, intimidated by the level of opulence in the big vehicle. 'I believed that you worked for Millwrights—'

'No, I own Millwrights. They run audits for me,' Aristide told her casually. 'I did wonder what was happening this morning when nobody appeared for my benefit, but your charming company was a plus and I let it go.'

Tabby breathed in deep and slow, steadying her nerves. 'Then may I ask why you were at Traxis today?'

'I bought it over—'

'Traxis?' Tabby gasped in surprise and consternation because it was an international company. 'You *own* it?'

Good heavens, had she allowed herself to be chatted up by her new employer?

'If you're my boss, I shouldn't be here with you!' Tabby exclaimed in dismay. 'If you stop the car, I'll get out here—'

Aristide studied her in wonderment. 'Are you mad? I'm not your boss. I won't be taking much of an active part in running Traxis. My role is behind the scenes. I buy companies, reorganise them and then move on to the next,' he explained levelly.

Her heart still beating very fast at the belief that she was not only way out of her depth with such a guy but also doing something wrong in going out with him, Tabby stared back at him anxiously. 'I'm still not sure I should be with you—'

A big lean brown hand closed over hers where she had braced her own on the seat. 'Relax, *angelos mou*,' he urged. 'Of course you should be with me tonight. It's what you want…and what I want. Why should anything else come into it?'